The Death of the Admiral

A Nathan Tower Novel of Espionage and Intrigue

Jim Stovall

First Inning Press

ISBNs:

Ebook : 978-1-968176-03-7
Paperback: 978-1-968176-04-4
Hardback: 978-1-968176-05-1

Contents

Sign up for Jim's newsletter

ONE OF THE BEST ways of staying in touch with me is to get on my email list. You can do so at my website, .

My monthly newsletter will keep you informed about what I am doing and what I am writing about. There are also **extras** and **freebies**. For instance, if you read this book and are familiar with Nashville, particularly east Nashville, you will want to check out the interactive map that identifies some of the locations referred to in the book. There's a bit of extra information about them that will be of interest to you.

Also, by signing up for my newsletter, you can download a free digital copy of the mystery novel *Kill the Quarterback*, which is also set in Nashville. In *Kill the Quarterback*, a star quarterback is murdered two weeks before his senior season is about to begin. **Mitch Sawyer**, police reporter for the Nashville Daily Tribune, has to find the killer before he becomes the next victim.

Reviewers have had this to say about **Kill the Quarterback**:

"Shades of Damon Runyon . . . . Stovall writes about Nashville, where he grew up, and has a cast of characters to rival Runyon, but with a 21st century realism that Runyon would know nothing of."

"Every time I thought I had it all figured out there would be a new twist in the plot. Didn't put it down from start to finish."

"Stovall does a stellar job of character development as police reporter Mitch Sawyer digs into the murder, using sources and adversaries in Nashville's criminal justice system. Stovall uses his background in journalism to weave in insights into the changing newspaper industry, and his familiarity with Nashville to infuse color and a sense of familiarity into the story."

"A great story told from a different perspective than most mysteries ... the perspective of a newspaper reporter. Jim Stovall has woven a great story around some very intriguing characters. Enjoyed the book immensely, and looking forward to more stories from Jim."

1: The Summons

MEADE MEADOWS TURNED FROM 14th Street onto E Street and headed east, still clutching a piece of paper. The turn put him on what was popularly known as Rum Row in Washington, D.C., slowing him down due to the drunks, derelicts, and merrymakers that populated that block in the nation's capital. He was late. He pulled his watch from his waistcoat pocket.

Five minutes after midnight.

The street was raucous and noisy. A horse-drawn hansom cab clopped along the cobblestones, adding its discordant music to the general din and iniquity. The smell of alcohol—both consumed and waiting to be consumed—mixed with cigar smoke and the filth that seeped from the buildings.

The note he held was from Admiral Ezra Radford. It had been typed, but the admiral's unmistakable signature was scrawled at the bottom:

"Be at my office around midnight. Important."

Earlier that afternoon, the note had appeared on Meade's desk at the *Washington Beacon* office. Who had actually written it, and who delivered it, Meade had no idea. He couldn't imagine the admiral using a typewriter. It had to be one of his clerks, but that was not the mystery Meade needed to solve right then.

Why his office—why at midnight? What could he possibly want?

Meade had met the admiral several times but did not know him well. He remembered the first conversation they had ever had.

"I know your father, my boy," the admiral had said.

"Yes, sir," Meade replied.

The admiral had a voice that sounded as if he were always calling out orders aboard ship. *"If you're half the man he is, well, you'll be all right."* Everybody in the room had heard that.

It wasn't the first time since he had come to Washington to work as a journalist that he had heard that kind of thing. Hubert Meadows was the kind of man who knew everyone, especially everyone in Washington. That's one of the reasons—probably the main reason—that Meade left home. But escaping his father, he found, was not that easy.

Why midnight? Why not daylight hours? Why me?

Once he made it past the Imperial Hotel, the National Theater, and the string of bars and bawdy houses that continued for another block and a half, the darkness and sudden silence began to envelop him. A sense of foreboding crept into his mind. *Something's not right,* he thought. *Maybe, just maybe, this is normal for the old admiral. Maybe he works late. Maybe this is when he normally sees people.*

Meade tried to use these speculations to combat the dread creeping up his spine and into his thinking.

The admiral was part of the Office of Naval Intelligence, a unit created as part of the Navy's expansion and modernization program begun in 1882. As a Washington journalist, Meade had watched this expansion take place over the last three years. He had even written a few stories about it, but it had never been high on his agenda.

Still, he shared his father's trait—for good or ill—of meeting and getting to know a wide variety of people. His circle of friends and sources of information expanded daily. Meade was a good reporter, and his wide network only strengthened his skills.

The admiral's office was in a building a block away. It was an old three-story structure that the government had acquired mainly to house the ever-expanding Patents Office. Few people knew the Navy kept an office in the building.

Meade remembered a brief conversation he had had with the admiral. He had asked the old man why, when the United States seemed to be under no threat from any country, the nation's leaders had decided to build up the military.

"You write stories about the State Department, don't you, son?" the old admiral had said. Meade acknowledged that he did so. *"So, I guess you think that this world is full of friends of the United States. That's what they seem to think over at State."*

"The State Department is full of people who are diplomats. I guess they're just trying to get along with everybody else," Meade answered. The admiral nodded in agreement. *"You're probably right. That's their job. What you have to understand is that in the military, our job is just the opposite. We look upon everybody as a potential enemy."*

As Meade thought about that snippet of conversation, he wondered if it might have something to do with his midnight meeting with the admiral. He checked his watch again.

Ten minutes after midnight.

Meade quickened his step. The note had said *"around midnight."* Whatever that meant, Meade was certain that he was now late. Being late didn't sit well with people in the military—especially admirals.

The building that held the admiral's office was dark except for one light coming from a window on the third floor. It had to be the admiral's office. Meade bounded up the stairway from the street to the front door, expecting to confront a night watchman. Instead, the door was partially open, and a long, dark hallway lay before him. Night watchmen usually made periodic rounds during their shifts, so the absence of one at the door was nothing unusual. They didn't often leave the doors unlocked, however.

The end of the hallway led to a stairwell that would take him up to the third floor. Meade walked carefully down the hallway, adjusting his eyes to the dim lighting and trying to listen for any sounds that might provide him with some kind of information about where he was. He saw little and heard only his own footsteps on the wooden floor.

On the landing of the third floor, Meade was met with another long hallway. Darkness obscured every detail that the hallway's doors and signs might have furnished. The only light came from a transom at the far end of the hall. It was obvious to Meade that this was the same light he had seen from the street.

Before venturing into the darkness, Meade stopped walking and held his breath, listening for any sound. He heard nothing, but the silence did not convince him that he was alone. Somebody was in that building besides the admiral in his office.

Meade walked carefully along the hallway, his eyes wide open to take in as much light as possible. When he reached the door below the lighted transom, he could make out the sign on the door: **Admiral Ezra Radford.**

Meade knocked, a loud, resounding knock that echoed down the hallway. There was no response. He knocked again, with the same result.

"Admiral Radford," he said. "It's Meade Meadows."

No response.

Meade took a deep breath, grabbed the door handle, and gave it a twist. There was no lock, and the door opened easily.

Then Meade saw what he had feared—though he hadn't been able to picture or name it.

The admiral was sitting in his chair, but his head and chest were slumped over onto the desk. The desk was a large one, and Meade knew his woods well enough to know the top was red oak. The admiral's left hand and arm were also on the desk, and near that hand lay a pistol. A stream of blood was pooling under the admiral's head.

2: The Admiral's Office

"*M*EIN *GOTT*," MEADE MEADOWS muttered under his breath. It was one of the few German expressions he knew, and he had taught himself to say it whenever he was surprised, shocked, or horrified. It was also a signal to himself to stop—to stop talking, if that was what he was doing. To stop thinking, as much as he could. To take a deep breath. To look, to listen, to breathe.

The scene before him had one overriding fact: the old admiral was dead. That was something he would deal with momentarily. Right now, however, Meade's job was to ignore that fact and take in everything else he could see, hear, and understand.

You are not part of this, he told himself. *You are a witness and observer. What is before you is incomprehensible. It's your job to comprehend it.*

As he surveyed the room, a wave of unease washed over him. The admiral's death was too sudden, too unexpected. Meade had always admired the admiral's sharp mind and unwavering dedication. The idea that such a formidable figure could be reduced to a lifeless body sprawled across his desk was unsettling.

The admiral's desk was littered with papers, books, pens, and the paraphernalia the old man apparently liked to keep close when he worked. At first glance, it seemed the items were randomly scattered—some had even fallen to the floor. Something about the desk struck Meade as odd but familiar.

Later, he told himself. *I'll think about that later. Now is the time to take in and remember as much as possible.*

While he was looking at the desk, Meade was listening closely. Footsteps, down the hall. They started slowly, and then picked up speed. A noticeable change in the sound came when the footsteps hit the stairway—now they were running.

Meade's first instinct was to run down the hallway and follow, but something about the rhythm of those steps told him he'd never catch up. It would be a waste of effort and time. He would find himself on an empty street with no idea which way to go.

What could he tell from the sound? The footsteps weren't loud or lumbering. Whoever they belonged to was light-footed—and likely lightweight.

Time. He didn't have much. He needed to use what he had. Instinctively, Meade knew he did not want to be found in the admiral's office with the old man lying there dead. The night watchman would be making his rounds soon, and Meade needed to be someplace else when that happened.

He stepped further into the office—two steps forward, then stopped. The shift in position offered a new perspective. The office was larger than he'd imagined. The admiral's desk sat near the windows facing E Street. On the opposite side of the office was a large conference table surrounded by chairs. The interior walls were lined with bookshelves and cabinets, some with doors, some open. In one corner stood an assistant's desk with more cabinets beside it.

Meade turned back to the admiral. What was he looking at? A suicide, a murder, an accident? At first glance, it looked like suicide.

But something about the scene didn't sit right. Meade, for reasons he couldn't yet explain, believed wholeheartedly that someone else had been in the room when the admiral died.

A chill ran up his spine. His instincts, which he trusted, were screaming that this was no ordinary death. The admiral had enemies—plenty of them—and Meade couldn't shake the feeling that one of those enemies had finally taken their revenge.

He moved to the desk. Books, papers, maps, and official-looking documents covered its surface. A navigational chart of an unidentifiable region had fallen to the floor, likely dropped when the admiral slumped over. Among the clutter were technical schematics of a new naval vessel and a personal letter from a high-ranking official. An old, leather-bound journal was partially hidden under a stack of reports.

Mounted on a wooden stand behind the desk was a ship's bell—likely from a vessel the admiral had once commanded. It was well-polished, and the clapper was clearly visible. The sound of that bell, Meade thought, could probably fill the entire block if rung properly.

He picked up the chart and, without quite knowing why, stuffed it into his pocket. Then he scanned the desk again—carefully avoiding the head, torso, and blood—and looked for anything that might offer a clue. One document bore the letterhead of the German Embassy. Beside it lay a photograph of the admiral with several men—some of whom Meade recognized as key figures in the Navy.

Just as he was about to pick up the German Embassy letter, he heard footsteps from the far end of the hallway.

The night watchman.

Meade glanced around the office. The light would already have been seen—it was too late to switch it off. Within seconds, the watchman would be inside the room and would find the body.

He needed a hiding place.

He slipped behind the assistant's desk, squeezing himself between it and the wall.

The door opened. A sharp gasp. Then came a string of expletives, followed by the sound of footsteps moving toward the admiral's desk. More expletives.

In a moment of panic, Meade thought about the bell. *What if he sees it and rings it?* The loud, resonant sound would alert everyone nearby. The room would soon be filled with people.

He held his breath.

Then footsteps again. Louder, heavier—retreating.

The watchman had run.

Meade heard him pounding down the stairs. A moment later, he was on E Street, blowing his whistle and shouting for help.

Meade wasted no time. He darted from the office, down the back stairway. At the bottom, he found a door leading to a rear exit and out into an alleyway. Once outside, he paused, drawing in the cool night air.

3: Burley O'Malley

B URLEY O'MALLEY KNEW HOW to savor a beer. He enjoyed the taste, smell, texture, and overall good feeling with every swallow. He knew his grog and enjoyed it.

"One thing I know," he told Meade, "is that the old man didn't kill himself."

"How do you know that?" Meade asked.

"'Cause I know the old man, that's how. Served with him when we were fighting the Rebs, and long after that. The old man was good, no doubt about that."

"A good commander?"

"A good cap'n and a good man. Best there was," Burley said, taking another full drink from his glass. "Some of those captains and admirals weren't worth spit—but not the old man."

Meade and Burley sat across from each other at a small table in the Townhouse Saloon. Meade glanced at his watch. It was just after one o'clock, barely an hour since he had been in the admiral's office.

++

Meade had left the office building and worked his way through a couple of dark alleys before he felt it safe to go a half block south and back onto E Street. Along the way, Meade stopped a few times to make vague sense of what he had just seen. His vision of the admiral's office and the admiral's dead body had a surreal quality. He knew what he had seen—that had been real enough—but nothing in his experience or knowledge could make sense of it.

The admiral was a prominent figure. He had been around and well-known for a long time. Undoubtedly, he had enemies. Who they might be, and what the source of their enmity toward the admiral was, Meade simply could not discern.

The alley Meade was attempting to negotiate was dark and unfamiliar. Moving quickly but quietly, he pushed thoughts of the admiral aside to focus on what he could see—and what he might not be able to see—right in front of him. He needed a place to stop and think. He knew he could find that place when he made it back to E Street.

He could hear the night watchman's whistle. It was answered by one, then two, then three police whistles.

Once on E Street, Meade kept to the doorways and shadows to avoid being noticed. He didn't have to worry. All eyes were on the two hefty policemen racing down the middle of the street toward the admiral's office. Meade ducked into the Townhouse Saloon, a seedy little joint he knew—and didn't like. But it was the perfect place to be on this particular night.

The Townhouse Saloon was a hole-in-the-wall fixture of E Street, catering to drunks, derelicts, and the generally down and out. The dimly lit, long, narrow room offered Meade exactly what he needed: a place to hide and a place to watch without being watched. The saloon was almost empty, and Meade surmised that most of its customers were out on the street listening, absorbing, and interpreting the latest news—the death of Admiral Radford.

The large bartender with a thick handlebar mustache gave Meade a look that clearly said, *What's a tight-ass like you doing in a place like this?* Meade ignored the message and sent one of his own.

"Give me a Ballantine beer, and make sure it's in a clean glass." Meade held the bartender's stare until the barkeep knew he wasn't kidding.

"How much?" Meade asked.

The bartender told him.

Meade dug out twice that amount from his pocket and put it on the bar. "Keep it," he said.

Meade took his beer and found an empty table toward the back of the bar. The odors of cigar smoke, alcohol, and less-than-pristine male human beings mixed together to give the place its unappealing ambiance. The walls featured posters for prizefights, laxative medicines, and circus acts pinned up against the peeling paint. The mismatched tables and chairs had seen too many of their own prizefights and brawls.

Meade was still not ready to fully assess what he had seen in the admiral's office. He decided to watch, wait, and see what the street deposited into this little corner of hell. The one conclusion he had come to in the last fifteen minutes was that, at least for the moment, he was not going to tell anyone that he had been in the admiral's office and had discovered the body. That fact was his and his alone.

++

Meade's watching and waiting was soon rewarded when a group of drunken sailors stumbled into the saloon, intent on reaching a higher level of inebriation than they had already attained. The admiral's demise had offered them the perfect excuse.

"So, the old boy topped himself," one said.

"That's what one copper said."

"That's not what I heard. I heard he was murdered."

"Who would murder old Radford? I never thought he was worth killing."

"Did the cops say they had caught anybody?"

"There's nobody to catch, you idiot. He topped himself. Cop says they found the gun right beside him."

"Some guy told me he was in a gunfight and got the worst of it."

The drunken speculation went on for fifteen or twenty minutes. The beer flowed freely through the conversation. The murder was solved, the suicide confirmed, the gunfight had witnesses, and the police had a suspect in custody. Each of these "facts" was stated unequivocally and without much in the way of attribution.

Meade took it all in from his back-of-the-bar table. When the conversation finally lapsed, Meade noticed that one of the sailors seemed older and quieter than the rest. He was a short, stocky, confident man who knew how to handle himself physically and emotionally. Another member of the group suggested that they all head down the street toward the admiral's office to see what was going on.

Meade eyed the older sailor and got his attention. As the others got up to leave, Meade, as unobtrusively as he could, walked over to the man and said, "Fancy a Ballantine beer?"

"That's not a cheap drink, friend."

"I'm guessing from what you didn't say," Meade replied, "that you knew the admiral."

The man nodded.

"Then I'd say the admiral at least deserves the best beer this place has to offer," Meade said.

The man nodded again. He stuck out his hand, and Meade shook it.

"My name is Meade Meadows."

"Burley O'Malley. People call me Pops," he said, the beer untouched between them.

4: Gunnery Mate

T HE LINES AND WRINKLES on Burley O'Malley's weather-beaten face told Meade Meadows one story, while Burley sat at the table sipping his Ballantine beer and telling a not dissimilar tale in his own unique voice.

"Been at sea since I was twelve years old," Burley said in his gravelly voice. "If I counted 'em up, bet I spent more of my days on the water than on solid earth. But who's counting? Sure ain't me."

Meade let him talk, listening intently. It was what made him a good reporter. He listened and kept his mouth shut. Meade had an ear for what people were really saying. Sometimes it was the opposite of the words they used, but he could understand and take it in like few others could.

"Ain't no girl ever tempted me out of the Navy," Burley said with a chuckle. "Plenty of 'em tried, let me tell you."

Burley was bragging, and Meade let him brag. He knew interrupting a man who was trying to tell you something about himself was a mistake.

"Twelve years old?" Meade knew how to direct a conversation without asking a real question.

Burley said that his Irish immigrant parents came to Boston with three kids, and he was the fourth. "Born in America," he said. When he was about nine, both parents died of cholera, and an uncle who was supposed to care for them kicked him out of the house. "I guess I was a little wild back then."

Burley survived on the streets for a couple of years until one day he saw a U.S. Navy ship pull into port. "I decided right then I needed to change the scenery. Stowed myself away under a lifeboat, and the ship had been out to sea for a couple of days before they found me. Was I hungry! Them guys laughed at me so hard 'cause I ate and ate and ate. One of them said we're gonna have to pull in somewhere and get extra provisions just to feed this kid."

"But they took care of you?"

"Damn right they did—better than any family ever had. And you know who was a midshipman on board that vessel? Ezra Radford, that's who."

The noise of the Townhouse Saloon ebbed and flowed depending on whether the drunks were coming or going. The excitement that the admiral's death had generated was all but gone. It was nearly 2:00 a.m., and he was just another topic of conversation.

Meade kept his eye on the door, not knowing exactly what to expect but expecting something. Then it happened: a big, strapping, uniformed policeman walked in. He was holding a nightstick and had the look of someone eager to use it. The saloon fell silent immediately.

The policeman walked over to the bartender, placed his nightstick on the bar, stared at the bartender, and waited. The bartender stared back, but everyone knew what his next move would be. He reached under the bar and came up with a large, clean glass. He hit one of the taps, and the beer flowed into the glass with a gush. He then set the glass in front of the policeman, bringing it down on the bar—possibly a little too loudly.

The policeman stared back at him, then looked down at the glass and the beer. "Thanks, barkeep," he said.

He picked up the glass, held it to his mouth, and five seconds later, the glass was empty. Then he let it drop on the floor, and it smashed into a thousand pieces. The barkeeper didn't move, didn't flinch, and didn't say a word.

Finally, the policeman spoke. "Anybody been in here tonight unusual or suspicious?" His tone was harsh, and his volume was above average. He continued to stare at the barkeeper.

Meade expected the barkeeper to turn his head and nod toward him. Instead, the barkeeper kept looking at the policeman and finally said in an even tone, "Nobody you'd be interested in."

Meade realized at that moment that there was one thing the barkeeper hated more than people like him who shouldn't be there. He hated policemen.

The cop picked up his nightstick, spat on the floor, and walked out.

The noise in the bar resumed before the door had shut.

Meade saw that the glasses in front of Burley and him were empty. He grabbed them and took them to the bar. "Another round," he said, "and thanks." When the glasses had been filled, Meade laid down a ten-dollar bill on the bar. The two beers, he calculated, were worth about 25 cents apiece. The rest was for services rendered.

The barkeeper nodded and, without a word, picked up the bill and stuffed it in his pocket. As Meade headed back to the table with his beers, the barkeeper picked up a broom and started sweeping up the broken glass.

Burley was glad to have a fresh beer in front of him. He took a long, slow sip.

"Cops," he said with disgust. "Most of them would rather **crack skulls** than take a warm bath."

"You've had your run-ins, I suppose," Meade said.

Burley nodded. "Cops seem to like to keep their nightsticks in practice by laying them across the head of a sailor. That's happened to me a couple of times, but not lately."

"So the lads on your first ship treated you pretty good?"

Burley grinned. "Yeah, they were okay."

"What about Ezra Radford?"

"Two things I remember about the admiral from that first voyage. Two things that changed my life. One day some of the lads decided it'd be fun to get me drunk, so they kept feeding me grog and laughing and having a big time of it. The admiral—of course, then he wasn't an admiral, just a midshipman—stepped in and stopped them. Then he gave me a lecture about drinking too much. He wasn't a prohibitionist or anything like that. He just said, 'The grog will get you if you let it.'"

"What was the other thing?"

Burley took a deep breath. "He taught me to read. That wasn't easy, 'cause I was in no particular mood to learn. But he stuck with it and stuck with me and taught me anyway. To this day, I don't know why he did that. He had plenty of other stuff to do, but he paid a lot of attention to me. Nobody had ever done that before."

Meade and Burley sat there for a little while in silence. Meade kept listening to see if he could pick up something from some of the other conversations going on in the saloon. He didn't hear anything worth noting.

"Somewhere along the way," Burley said, "I decided the Navy

was my life. When I was old enough, I joined up officially and got assigned to a warship where I was trained as a gunnery mate. Sometimes things happen that are meant to happen."

"What do you mean?"

"Well, I got really interested in ordnance and armaments and the kinds of guns the Navy was putting on board ships. I somehow figured out—unlike most of the rest of the lads—that the Navy was a war machine, and when a war came, the guns and the ordnance were going to be at the center of it. And that's where I wanted to be."

When the Confederates fired on Fort Sumter in 1861, everything changed, according to Burley. At least, everything should have changed. The problem, he told Meade, was that it didn't change fast enough, and the changes weren't widespread enough to get ahead of what the rebels were doing.

The bureaucrats in Washington dibbled and dabbled and spent their time on spontoons when they should have been figuring out how to build more ships and supply them. Burley said that finally happened—but it took too long.

One of the things the Navy did right, however, according to Burley, was to recognize the importance of armor and armaments and to identify the sailors who knew the most about that. One of those sailors, Burley said, was him. He got assigned to several ships and shore stations and became well known in the middle ranks as being able to fire any kind of gun or cannon at any kind of target and figure out quickly how to do it.

"I even studied small arms and made the argument that officers ought to give up their swords and carry rifles and pistols instead." He laughed. "You can imagine how well that went over."

Still, Burley said he was assigned to the USS *Kearsarge* in 1863, and the chief mission of that ship was to find and destroy the *CSS Alabama*, which had been wreaking havoc on American shipping for many months. The *Alabama* was commanded by Raphael Semmes, who cut a romantic and dashing figure with the world's press.

"Our chief mission was to find the *Alabama* and put it at the bottom of the ocean, preferably with Semmes tied to the main mast," he said. "We just about did that too."

Burley talked about tracking the *Alabama* into the English Channel and trapping her in the harbor at Cherbourg, France.

"We knew we had her, and we knew there wasn't nothing she could do but come out and put up a fight."

Burley told Meade about the *Kearsarge*'s secret weapon. They had forged a set of chains that they had dropped over the side of the ship to protect her from battering cannonballs from the enemy. They had disguised those chains by putting up boards to simulate the appearance of a wooden ship. Burley was in charge of one of the main battery units, and his commanding officer for that unit was none other than Ezra Radford, who by then had reached the rank of lieutenant commander.

"The *Alabama* never had a chance," Burley said. "When she came out of that harbor, we made quick work of her. The battle was fierce, but it wasn't long. There were three cheers when we saw her start to go down."

Burley O'Malley stopped and took a long drink from his beer. "But let me tell you something," he said. "I'm no respecter of persons. I respect men who earn it. Raphael Semmes was an enemy, and he was a brave man. We were out there to kill him and he knew that.

And he gave it everything he had. So I respect him."

Burley looked at Meade, and Meade saw tears in his eyes.

"But you know what? That's all changed."

"What do you mean?" Meade asked.

"Today's Navy ain't about brave men and ain't about sailing ships. It's about bureaucrats and spies and liars and men who don't know how to fight. Radford knew that, and that's one of the reasons he got killed."

5: I Know Who You Are

"**I** KNOW WHO YOU are," Burley O'Malley said.

Burley O'Malley and Meade Meadows had lapsed into a comfortable silence. They were both surprised at how easy it felt to be in each other's company without speaking. The Townhouse Saloon had grown quiet; most of the drunks had left, and the few who remained seemed content to sit quietly.

Meade stuck out his hand. "Meade Meadows. I write for the *Washington Beacon*."

"How do you know who I am?" Meade asked.

Burley grinned—a beer-filled grin—and said, "You're that guy who caught the president's killer."

Meade shook his head. "That's not how it happened."

"That's what all the papers said. That's what everybody was talking about for a long time. I remember that."

"I didn't catch the president's killer. I just bumped into him. It was the policeman who grabbed him."

"Speaks well of a fella who won't take credit for what he done," Burley said.

Meade hadn't expected this topic to come up. It had been nearly five years ago. He rarely thought about the incident and assumed others had too. Occasionally, as with his conversation with Burley

O'Malley, the topic would present itself, and the story inevitably cast him as the hero. No matter how much he insisted otherwise, people attributed his denial to modesty.

Meade had just come to Washington and started work at the *Washington Beacon* as a cub reporter. He had been sent to the Baltimore and Potomac Railroad Station because the editors had heard that President James Garfield, who had been in office for only a few months, was about to leave town for a vacation. They thought it would be good for a young reporter like Meade to see if he could grab a few words with the president.

Meade was walking through the door of the train station when he caught sight of the president, who was already inside. The president was talking with a couple of his political cronies, one of whom Meade recognized as James G. Blaine, then Secretary of State. Meade called out, "Mr. President," loud enough that Garfield began to turn toward him.

At that very moment, a man emerged from the crowd behind the president, pointed a gun to his head, and fired twice. Meade was within ten feet of the action and instinctively lunged toward the man with the gun. The assassin, Charles J. Guiteau, turned toward Meade and started to walk toward the exit. Within seconds, they collided. Meade lost his balance, but the assassin kept moving forward. Without thinking, Meade grabbed onto his coat—an action that did not stop him but slowed him down.

Meade remembered *feeling the coat give way. Whether it was tearing or simply coming off,* he did not know. *What was without a doubt in Meade's recollection was that Guiteau was slipping away from him.* In no way had he "caught" the assassin. That task was performed a few seconds later when a Washington policeman grabbed Guiteau and threw him to the floor.

The president had been badly wounded, and the attention of just about everyone in and around the station was fixed on him. He was quickly rushed back to the President's Mansion, and Meade was able to escape the station without much notice.

When Meade returned to the offices of the *Washington Beacon*, the editors and reporters had already heard what had happened to the president. What they did not know was the minor role Meade had played in the whole drama. When Meade told them what he had seen and done, the editors were ecstatic. One of them told him, "Every newspaper in this country has the story of the attempt on Garfield's life. But only the *Washington Beacon* has you."

Meade was ordered to write up in great detail what he had seen and done. When he turned in his story, the editors quickly rewrote most of it to place him at the center of the action and make him their own local hero. The next day's edition of the paper carried a long account of the shooting that focused more on Meade than it did on either the president or his would-be assassin. The paper also carried a large photograph of Meade.

The next few weeks, as far as Meade was concerned, were hell on earth. Everywhere he went, people wanted to shake his hand, buy him a drink, or hear the story from his own mouth. He became a reluctant celebrity, his face and name recognized by strangers in the street. It was a level of attention he neither wanted nor enjoyed. The fame brought expectations he didn't want and pressures he wasn't ready for. *He had come to Washington to be a reporter, not a hero.*

Burley wanted to talk about what it was like to catch the man who had shot the president. Meade had been through this conversation many times before, and he was irritated to have to talk about it again.

But Meade knew enough by now to understand that those who wanted to talk about the incident didn't necessarily want the truth. *They wanted the hero story straight from the hero's mouth.*

Meade would give them as much of that as he could while remaining within the broad bounds of honesty. In Burley's case, Meade wanted to keep him talking—not about James Garfield or Charles Guiteau, but about what Burley might know about the death of the admiral.

They talked. When Burley seemed satisfied with the hero story, Meade gently steered him back—to the Navy, the admiral, and Burley himself. His mind raced as he considered how best to steer the conversation. The transition needed to be seamless, almost natural, to keep Burley engaged and willing to share more. Meade's curiosity about Admiral Radford's death was more than professional—it was personal. He had admired Radford from afar, impressed by his reputation and dedication. The news of his sudden demise had struck a chord in Meade, stirring a mix of grief and determination to uncover the truth.

They talked for a few minutes about Burley's time on the *USS Kearsarge*. Burley clearly didn't mind expanding on that topic.

"I'll tell you what," he said, "and there ain't nobody you know who can contradict it, but we had the best gunnery unit in the whole Navy. In fact, it was the best in anybody's Navy."

"And Ezra Radford was your unit commander," Meade said.

"Right you are, and a good one too. Best there was. We were in the middle of the action, right where we wanted to be, but the commander—he took care of us. He made sure that we didn't get overheated and that we weren't exposed to unnecessary fire."

"And that was unusual?"

"Damn right it was unusual. Back then, most of the officers didn't give a damn about the men who served under them. We were just cannon fodder. But the admiral, he would go to bat for us, make sure we had the things we needed—the ammunition, the water, everything we needed to load up those eleven-pounders and put fire on the enemy's deck. He was right there with us the whole time."

"What about after the war was over? Did you see him much after that?"

Burley explained that at the end of the war, most of the sailing crews wanted to get to shore as quickly as possible and get mustered out of the Navy.

"They had this big idea," he said, "that they were going to take their Navy pay, head west, and strike it rich. I knew better than that. Ships were decommissioned all over the place, and the Navy that we knew fighting the Rebs became a shadow of itself. But I stuck with it. So did the admiral."

"So you two maintained contact all through those lean years, right?"

Burley nodded. "I saw the admiral a lot during those years. Occasionally we had assignments together. He always took care of me, wanted to know how I was doing, wanted to know if I needed anything."

"What about lately? When's the last time you saw the admiral?"

Burley shrugged. "I can't rightly say. Probably hasn't been more than a month or so. I just stopped by his office to say hello, see how he was doing."

Meade thought this might be the end of their conversation, so he put the question to Burley that he had been waiting to ask all evening.

"How much do you know about what the admiral was involved in?"

"Oh, I know plenty," Burley said, leaning in closer, his voice dropping to a conspiratorial whisper. "Plenty."

Meade's pulse quickened. "Like what?"

Burley glanced around the saloon. At that point in the early morning, only a couple of other tables were occupied, and they were too far away to hear the whispers between Burley and Meade.

"The admiral—he was sailing in some deep and dangerous waters. He was one of those who wanted to change some stuff about the Navy, and he was running headlong into some powerful people who were just fine with the way things were."

"You mean corruption?" Meade said.

Burley hesitated. "Yeah, of course there was that. There's a guy in the supplies and provisions division named Jonathan Hayes. He and the admiral go way back—but not in a good way. Hayes was on the *Kearsarge* like the rest of us. He and the admiral never seemed to agree about anything."

Burley lowered his voice even more. "You want to look into something, Mr. Reporter, my money would be on that Hayes fella."

"You think that's what got the admiral killed?"

"Maybe."

Meade waited. Burley had something else to say.

"I think it went deeper than that, deeper than somebody just getting rich off the Navy stores. *Whatever it was got him killed—and whoever did it wouldn't stop with just the admiral. They'd want to take out anybody who stood in their way.*"

"Meaning somebody like me."

"Yeah, I guess that's what I mean."

Meade considered carefully what he had just heard. He let the words sink in and again waited to see if Burley had anything to add. Burley was looking at him intently but didn't seem like he was about to say anything.

"How do you know this?" Meade finally asked.

Burley looked nervously at his beer and then looked around the saloon. "I've said too much already," he said and stood up to leave. "I'll be in touch."

Meade watched Burley disappear into the early morning haze, wondering if he'd hear from him again.

6: The Diplomat

"SO, THE OLD ADMIRAL is dead."

The Diplomat looked at the beer in his less-than-clean glass and decided he'd had enough. The beer didn't suit him. Neither did the place. He was used to the lobbies, dining rooms, and bedrooms of the Willard Hotel—not this dingy, smelly, smoke-filled little E Street saloon.

He sat rigid in his rickety chair at a table sticky with old beer, tobacco juice, and residues of unknown origin. He was impeccably dressed in a morning suit with a carnation in the lapel. A mustache covered a quarter of his upper lip, each hair trimmed to within a millimeter of the others.

The American nodded, the motion barely perceptible beneath the dark robe and hood.

"Yes, he's dead."

Raucous laughter exploded from another part of the saloon, obliterating any conversation. The Diplomat winced, his nostrils flaring at the acrid smell of cheap tobacco and spilled whiskey.

"And this is the first part of your plan?" he asked, leaning in closer.

The American made a slight movement that the Diplomat interpreted as a shrug. It was hard to tell. The figure wore a dark robe with a hood, and a black, broad-brimmed hat obscured the face.

The Diplomat didn't know what the American looked like, and it unsettled him more than he cared to admit.

"There is a plan, but you know how plans can change." The American spoke in surprisingly fluent Spanish. The tone was low, quiet, and confident, with a hint of an accent the Diplomat couldn't quite place.

"What do you mean? I thought we had an agreement."

"We have an agreement," the American said. "I have the plan."

The Diplomat stood on the edge of irritation. The American was always saying things like this—misdirecting, hinting at something.

For this, the Diplomat thought to himself, *I am up in the middle of the night, in a place like this saloon. For this, I left the bed of a young and beautiful woman—the wife of an aging United States senator. A woman whose lovemaking was not only active but at times aggressive. A woman who knows secrets I must discover for the good of my country.*

He took a deep breath, his irritation cooling as he reminded himself of the larger stakes at play. Spain's hold on the Americas was slipping—and with the U.S. expanding its naval power, the stakes had never been higher.

If the American read his thoughts, there was no sign. The brim of the hat covered one eye; the other eye, dark and unreadable, stared directly at him.

"The money," the American said, a gloved hand emerging from the folds of his robe.

Ah, the money. Yes, of course. I should have known.

The Diplomat reached inside his brocaded vest and pulled out an envelope. He placed it, not too quickly, into the open hand of his companion, carefully avoiding contact with the sticky and unclean tabletop.

Without a glance at the envelope, the American slipped it inside the heavy cape.

"Do you want to count it?"

The American made no movement other than placing his empty hand back on the table. Long, slender fingers tapped a silent rhythm on the wood.

"If you have cheated me," the American said, "you will see me only one more time—and then you will never see anyone again."

The American's tone made the Diplomat's throat go dry. Despite his earlier disgust, he took a sip of his beer. Strangely, it helped him gather himself and his thoughts. He didn't need to be intimidated by this American. After all, the Diplomat represented one of the major powers in the world. America, despite its vastness and resources, was still a weak and backward nation. Its capital, this mud-soaked village named after a man who lived only in the last century, could not compare to the grandeur of London, Paris, Vienna, or Madrid.

He resumed the role for which he had been sent to this out-of-the-way place.

"No need for threats." He spoke smoothly, evenly, and, he was sure, convincingly. "We have just paid you a significant amount of money. We deserve to know some of the details of your plan."

"What details do you want to know?"

"You have confirmed that the admiral is dead."

The American nodded. The eyes in the face were still obscured, but the Diplomat sensed a hint of amusement in them.

Another explosion of laughter and shouting erupted in the saloon. The Diplomat waited patiently for it to subside, his fingers drumming on the sticky tabletop.

"This reporter you spoke of..."

"Meade Meadows," the American said, the name rolling off the tongue with a hint of familiarity that piqued the Diplomat's curiosity.

"Did he discover the body of the admiral as you had planned?"

"He did."

The Diplomat waited for more details, but none were forthcoming. He pressed on.

"So does he think the admiral committed suicide?"

"I don't know what he thinks," the American said. "I left the admiral's office looking like the old man had done himself in. Maybe that's what Meadows will conclude."

"Tell me about this Meade Meadows."

It was the American's turn to sound irritated. "I thought it was your business to stay informed about this place."

The Diplomat remained silent. Of course, he was familiar with Meade Meadows—the man who had captured the assassin of the president. But his inquiry had provoked an interesting and possibly revealing response from the American.

"Meadows works for the *Washington Beacon* newspaper," the American said with some exasperation. "The plan is for him to report the admiral's death as a suicide. If he does—knowing the way he approaches a story—he will need to give a reason."

The American paused before continuing. "And if he is as good as I think he is, he will pick up on the rumors about the admiral's dishonesty and treachery."

"Rumors that are not true."

"Rumors that I have taken some pains to spread. You wouldn't have to poke around much these days to hear there's a kickback scheme where the admiral had his finger in the pie. That's what I'm counting on our ace reporter to do."

"And if Meadows doesn't do this?"

Again, there was the slightest hint of a shrug from the American. That was followed by a few seconds of silence.

"Well, that's the problem with making plans. There are other people involved, and they don't always do what you want them to do."

"And what if that happens?"

"If that happens, you adjust your plans."

"Would that mean the elimination of Mr. Meadows?"

"It might. If he outlives his usefulness, he won't live much longer." The American's voice carried a chill that seemed to lower the temperature in the already cool saloon.

The conversation had veered off course. The Diplomat sought to return it to the main point.

"The fate of Meade Meadows is neither here nor there," he said with a flip of his wrist. "What we are interested in is the maps."

The American nodded. "On that, we agree. Meade Meadows is just the tool we use to find them."

The Diplomat left the saloon first and stepped into the cool night air. He stood straight and was glad to breathe air that was free of smoke and stale beer. He drew his golden watch out of his vest pocket. Nearly 3 a.m.

The American is difficult, he thought, *but maybe not that difficult.* He smiled to himself. He felt his interior coat pocket, assuring himself that the other envelope was still there. That envelope contained more money, just in case the American demanded extra payment. He also put his hand into the outside pocket of his coat. The small pistol, cold to the touch, remained there. Neither the envelope nor the pistol had been necessary tonight.

He took another deep breath.

If he could complete this operation successfully, his superiors would undoubtedly notice, and his next posting would be some major European capital. He dreamed of that. He dreamed of Paris or Vienna.

And in the quiet of the street, he allowed himself one final hope: that the beautiful woman would still be there when he returned.

7: Lucinda Meadows

THE SOLID RED OAK desk in Meade Meadows' study had once stood as a tree along the Cumberland River a few miles north of Nashville. It had been selected by Hubert Meadows, Meade's father, and processed by the Nashville Lumber Company, which Hubert owned. Once milled, the wood was crafted into a magnificent desk by the best carpenters and woodworkers available in the South. The desk was a gift from Hubert when Meade announced he was moving to Washington.

Meade hadn't wanted the desk, but Hubert insisted. As often happened, Hubert's wishes prevailed.

On the morning after the admiral's death, Meade sat behind that desk, examining the items he had taken from the admiral's office earlier that morning. The tall windows in the study let in shafts of late-morning light, casting long shadows across the thick carpet and tall bookshelves that lined the walls. The air was still, touched by the faint scent of ink and old paper.

It was nearly noon. After returning home from his nocturnal adventures, Meade had fallen into a deep sleep, ushered there by a blend of excitement, fatigue, and Ballantine beer.

He studied the items before him: a leather packet, several documents, a torn piece of paper with handwriting on it, and an unidentified navigational chart. Individually, each item might tell a story, but collectively they made little sense.

"You were out very late last night."

Meade looked up to see his sister, Lucinda, standing in the doorway, observing the items on his desk. He had expected her to come into the study, which was why he had left the door open.

"Yes, I was out late. Very late," he responded, without elaboration.

"And would this have anything to do with the admiral's death?"

That was the trouble with Lucinda. He could never discern her thoughts, yet she always seemed to unravel his. He thought it but remained silent.

Though Meade was nearly twenty-eight and considered handsome by some, he never saw himself that way. He viewed himself as ordinary—unusually clean-shaven for his time, almost always well-dressed, and slightly taller than average at six feet one inch.

Lucinda, three and a half years his junior, was undeniably beautiful. With her thick dark hair, large brown eyes, high cheekbones, and shapely lips, she turned heads effortlessly. She possessed a practical and scholarly mind and made no effort to conceal her intelligence.

Meade trusted Lucinda more than anyone else. When he had announced his plans to move to Washington, Lucinda declared she would join him. They both loved their father but could not fulfill his desire for them to stay in Nashville and manage the family lumber business. That responsibility would fall to their younger sister, Caroline, their father's favorite.

Hubert had been displeased by their decision to leave, though he was too pragmatic to let his disappointment cause a rift. He recognized that his forceful personality, despite helping him through many challenges, wouldn't sway his adult children's decision.

When Meade and Lucinda announced their departure, Hubert established a generous trust fund for each, ensuring they would be free from financial worries. That financial security had enabled them to purchase their home on Connecticut Avenue.

"Tell me everything," Lucinda commanded. "Begin at the beginning."

Meade started by describing his encounter with the derelicts and drunks on E Street as he made his way to the admiral's office. He admitted he had been late because dinner with a friend at the Ebbitt Grill had run long. Lucinda listened patiently, though she sensed Meade was straying from the core of his story.

He recounted the shock of discovering the admiral's body. Occasionally, Lucinda interjected with questions or comments to steer him back on course, but mostly she listened intently, fully engaged by his narrative. Her attentive manner was a testament to the close bond they had forged throughout their childhood and early adult years, and one of the reasons Meade had immense trust in her judgment.

"Describe him in detail," Lucinda said after Meade mentioned meeting Burley O'Malley.

"He's shorter than average," Meade replied, "with a tough, weather-beaten face. He's stocky but muscular. He looks like he could handle himself in a boxing ring or maneuvering an eleven-pound gun on a ship's deck."

"How did he carry himself?" she asked.

Meade paused, searching his memory. "He had an easy manner, seemed relaxed most of the time—but perhaps like a tightly wound spring underneath."

"Would you describe him as heavy-footed or light-footed?"

"Definitely light-footed. He's not very heavy, and now that you mention it, his movements seemed smooth and unhurried."

Meade didn't question why Lucinda was probing with such specifics. He knew there was a reason behind her methodical approach.

"Okay, tell me everything you remember that he said," Lucinda urged.

Meade did his best to recall their lengthy conversation, though he couldn't remember every detail or the exact sequence of their exchange. He recounted as much as he could, focusing on providing a comprehensive overview.

When Meade finished, Lucinda sat silently for a moment, gazing out at the bustling Connecticut Avenue. Turning back to Meade, she said, "You left out something very important."

Meade raised an eyebrow. "What did I leave out?" he asked, both surprised and slightly irritated.

Lucinda held his gaze for a moment before answering.

"Where is the note that summoned you to the admiral's office?"

8: The Navigational Charts

MEADE MEADOWS PAUSED FOR several seconds, trying to recall where he had placed the note. He rose from his desk and crossed to the sofa, where he had flung his coat after stumbling in at dawn. His search of the outer pockets came up empty. Relief washed over him as he felt a piece of paper in an inner pocket. Extracting it, he briefly glanced at the note and then looked up triumphantly.

"Here it is," he said.

Lucinda, silent until now, extended her hand. When Meade passed her the note, she laid it on the red oak desk and carefully smoothed it out, touching only its edges.

After studying the note for a moment, she asked, "Are you sure this is the Admiral's signature?"

Meade nodded. "I've seen the Admiral's signature on several documents, and this one looks authentic."

"The paper lacks any heading or designation indicating it came from the Admiral's office," she said. "Why did you think it was genuine?"

"I wanted to discuss this year's Navy expansion plans with the Admiral," Meade replied. "I had sent him a note several weeks ago requesting an interview."

"And you assumed this was his response?"

"Yes. It was an unusual response, but admirals sometimes have their quirks. I thought this was just one of those."

Lucinda lifted the paper to the light. "It does have the Navy's watermark," she observed, "but that alone doesn't verify its authenticity."

"That's true," Meade conceded. "But the fact that the Admiral was in his office and the light was on lends the note some credibility."

"Perhaps you're right," Lucinda said, softening slightly.

She then focused intently on the note. "The note has been typed—obviously on a Remington 2 typewriter. They're popular these days for their shift key feature, which allows switching from lowercase to uppercase."

"The Navy certainly has plenty of typewriters," Meade said.

"One unique aspect of typewriters is that each types slightly differently. For instance, this note's lowercase 'e' is slightly out of alignment. If we could find the machine this was typed on, we might discover who sent it."

"I assume it was one of the Admiral's clerks," Meade said.

"That would be easy to verify if needed," Lucinda replied.

She turned her attention to another item Meade had retrieved from the Admiral's office—the navigational chart. "What do you make of this?"

"I honestly don't know. It was on the floor and seemed important, so I took it," Meade admitted.

Lucinda examined the chart, which appeared to depict a coastline, marked with various numbers but lacking any explanatory labels. In one corner were the initials "SWW."

"I wonder what these initials stand for," she said.

"In my experience, such initials usually belong to the person who drew the chart or supervised its creation."

"Do you have any idea who 'SWW' could be?"

"Not a clue," he confessed.

As Lucinda pondered in silence, Meade took a closer look at the chart for the first time since retrieving it. "This chart is incomplete," he said. "Navigational charts usually show coastline contours, water depths, maybe even seabed types. This one lacks all that—it must be a draft."

"That might explain why it was left out. Perhaps it was one of several drafts," Lucinda speculated. "Did you notice any other charts near the Admiral's desk?"

"Yes, there might have been other charts like this one. They all had curled edges, as if frequently rolled and unrolled."

"That could be significant."

A pause filled the room as Meade absorbed a new realization. "These charts, even incomplete, contain data that would be invaluable to foreign navies. The fact they were left out in the open could suggest they were seen by whoever confronted the Admiral."

A soft knock at the door broke the rhythm of their conversation. A housemaid asked if they wanted lunch; both agreed without hesitation.

Meade checked his watch—it was past noon.

"You haven't been to the newspaper office yet, have you?" Lucinda said.

Meade shook his head. "I wanted to avoid that place, at least for a few hours. The Admiral's death is likely to be a big story, and you know how the *Beacon* tends to sensationalize anything that might have a lurid angle. If I'm there, the editors will likely assign me to write the main story."

Since the Garfield incident, the *Washington Beacon's* editors had considered Meade their best reporter—a reputation he had earned through hard work and consistent writing. But the Admiral's death was one story he wasn't ready to cover. Not yet.

The police investigating the death were likely to conclude it was a suicide. Meade wasn't convinced—but he also didn't want to share what he knew.

Meade explained all this to Lucinda, who nodded in agreement.

"You need to stay as far away from that story as possible," she said. "You haven't told anyone that you were in the Admiral's office early this morning, have you?"

"Not a soul," he said.

"Not even Burley O'Malley?"

Meade shook his head.

"Good. No one needs to know."

Meade heard the finality in her voice and knew better than to argue.

9: The Washington Beacon

A COPY BOY NAMED Billy Hargis pressed a freshly print-ed newspaper into Meade Meadows' hands as he walked through the door into the cacophonous newsroom. It was nearly 3 o'clock in the afternoon.

"Extra edition," Billy said.

"Thanks, Billy," Meade responded, spreading the paper with both hands. **EXTRA** was emblazoned across the top in 36-point type. Below, spanning the wide expanse of the newspaper, an 84-point headline declared: **SUICIDE ADMIRAL**.

Meade had anticipated this kind of treatment for the admiral's story; after all, sensationalism was *The Washington Beacon*'s hall-mark. *Mein Gott!* he hissed to himself. His blood began to boil as he muttered the German phrase under his breath—his internal signal to stop, take a breath, consider, and assess.

"Something wrong, Mr. Meadows?" Billy lingered, noticing Meade's discomfort.

"No, Billy. Everything is just fine," Meade replied, masking his emotions. "Thanks for the newspaper."

At that moment, a shout of "COPY!" echoed through the room,

and Billy dashed off in response.

Meade headed to his desk, located in a corner of the large newsroom next to a window overlooking 11th Street and down to Pennsylvania Avenue. From his third-floor vantage point, the most prominent building he could see was the *Washington Evening News* building. He watched the bustling street below—vehicles and people, each absorbed in their business.

Life goes on, he thought. *An admired admiral has just died, a man who served his country all his adult life, and yet, no one seems to notice.* Life goes on.

Meade took a moment to recall his conversation with Lucinda. *Keep the secret,* she had said repeatedly. *Don't let anybody know what you know. Not just yet.*

They had talked through lunch and well into the afternoon. Lucinda was more than a sibling; she was a confidante, a second brain—someone who could view any situation through a different lens. Bright and independent, Lucinda had always possessed a unique clarity of thought, and Meade relied on it.

He smiled, recalling another of her predictions: *We'll probably hear from Papa this afternoon.* Just like with Meade, Lucinda often anticipated their father's actions before he made them.

"Papa knew the admiral very well, didn't he?" she had asked.

"Indeed, he did," Meade replied.

"Well, when he hears about the admiral's death, he's going to be in touch. He's probably already wired half the people in Washington."

Meade hadn't thought much about his father in the last few hours, but Lucinda's instincts were rarely off. Hubert Meadows was not one to stand idly by during major events. He would be making calls, asking questions, and ensuring that the right people were informed. That was how Hubert operated.

Meade's reverie was abruptly interrupted by a shout from the middle of the newsroom.

"Meadows! Get yourself over here!"

The newsroom of *The Washington Beacon* was a den of smoke, noise, and chaos—conversations layered over ringing phones, clacking typewriters, and the ever-present drone of wire service machines. From below came the thunder of the printing presses, sending a low vibration through the floors. Even with many windows shut, street sounds crept in.

And yet, George Callahan's voice could slice through it all.

Meade didn't want to hear it—but he wasn't surprised. He'd known it was coming.

Callahan, managing editor of the *Beacon*, stood behind his desk, chomping on a huge black cigar and sipping from a coffee cup that everyone knew wasn't filled with coffee.

"Where the hell have you been?" Callahan barked as he weaved through desks toward the center of the room.

Meade did not like George Callahan—and as everyone in the newsroom knew, the feeling was mutual.

"We've got a big honking story and you decide it's your day off?" Callahan roared. The noise level in the newsroom dropped noticeably as everyone paused to listen.

As irritating as Callahan could be, Meade knew this wasn't the time for a shouting match. He had plenty of issues with how the admiral's death was being reported, but this wasn't the moment to raise them. He needed to stay calm, sidestep the provocation, and nudge the coverage toward something more skeptical—and more respectful.

Meade glanced at the coffee cup. "Enjoying today's brand?" he asked quietly, with a faint grin. The jab landed.

Flustered and momentarily speechless, Callahan hesitated.

Meade seized the opening. "Let's talk a bit about this story," he said, adopting a tone of curiosity rather than confrontation. "I think I may have some information to add."

Even though Meade and Callahan didn't particularly like each other, Meade considered their relationship a work in progress. Callahan, now in his fifties, had more years in the newspaper business than Meade had years on earth. He'd started in New York at the *Herald*, rising from newsboy to reporter to editor under the infamous James Gordon Bennett. That kind of experience deserved respect.

Their lives couldn't have been more different. Meade had grown up with money and education. Callahan had clawed his way up from the gutter. Meade hoped that someday they might meet in the middle.

"Jack!" George shouted, summoning Jack Reynolds, the reporter who had filed the admiral story.

Jack approached with visible swagger. Unlike Callahan, his resentment toward Meade was personal.

"Yeah, and I don't need help from a pretty-boy reporter," Jack sneered.

Stocky, blunt, and perpetually aggrieved, Jack resented Meade's looks, upbringing, and access—everything Jack believed he lacked.

George ignored the comment. Meade didn't bite. Jack was spoiling for a fight.

"Where did the story come from, Jack?" George asked.

"It came from the police. Everything in it is solid," Jack said.

"And the police are calling it a suicide?"

"Suicide, pure and simple."

"How many cops did you talk to?"

"Just the investigating officer. He gave me everything."

"You didn't talk to anyone in the Navy?" Meade asked.

"Hell no. Why should I have?"

"Because the guy who's dead was a damned admiral," George snapped, cigar clenched between his teeth.

Jack scowled.

"Listen, George, I know some folks in the Navy. I can reach out and see what they say," Meade offered, steering the conversation toward something more productive.

"What are they gonna know about it?" Jack muttered dismissively.

"They might have insights we need," Meade said firmly.

George nodded toward Jack. "Go talk to some other cops—not just the lead investigator. We need to do more digging."

That final directive was a small win for Jack—the story was still his. Reporters were territorial. But it was also what Meade wanted. He didn't want to write the lead story—not yet.

Jack shot Meade a cold glare as he returned to his desk. His anger simmered just beneath the surface.

10: The Admiral's Funeral

PLAIN AND SPARE, THE interior of the New York Avenue Presbyterian Church offered no threat to the magnificence of the European cathedrals Meade Meadows had visited in his young life. For all their size and opulence, he thought, those cathedrals often obscured what they were meant to reveal.

This church, with its modest furnishings, rows of open pews, and unadorned altar and pulpit, captured something purer. Meade had been inside this sanctuary dozens of times. When he needed spiritual renewal, this was where he came. When he had nowhere to go on a rainy Sunday morning, it was better than any hotel salon in Washington. And when he simply needed a quiet place to think during the week, the church's doors were always open.

Part of its appeal was that Abraham Lincoln had once worshipped here. The church even had a designated "Lincoln pew," where the president had supposedly sat during Sunday services.

Meade had revered Lincoln since boyhood, even growing up in secessionist Nashville. In this, he reflected his father's values more than he liked to admit.

"Lincoln is the only hope this nation has of surviving," Hubert Meadows had told anyone and everyone who would listen.

"Why is that, Papa?" Meade or Lucinda would inevitably ask.

Hubert expected the question—and they knew to ask it. It was part of the ritual.

"Because he believes in something," Hubert would say, "and he is willing to give everything for it."

Then would come a full Hubert-style dissertation on what Lincoln believed and why it was the right thing to believe. Like most of Hubert's lectures—and Meade remembered them as both numerous and endless—the old man allowed no interruptions, no dissent. Only *Yes, Papa* was permitted.

Meade checked his watch. The admiral's funeral was set to begin in less than thirty minutes, but the sanctuary was still nearly empty.

Over the past few days, Meade had spoken with people both inside and outside the Navy. A general assumption had taken hold: the admiral had committed suicide. No one offered specific reasons or evidence—only vague sentiments like, *He must've had a lot on his mind,* or, *I guess he just couldn't take it anymore after all the action he'd seen.*

Yet a quiet disapproval hovered. Suicide, whatever the cause, was seen as weakness—something a naval officer should not commit. And that was where curiosity seemed to stop. No one seemed to know—or want to know—more.

That silence is suspicious, Meade thought. *How many people are going to show up today?*

He took a seat on the right side of the sanctuary, more than halfway toward the back. A reporter's seat, he thought—good for seeing without being seen. From there, he could observe who entered, who greeted whom, who made eye contact—and who avoided it.

At first, only a few people trickled in. The wooden floors and pews amplified every footstep and whisper. Some wore full dress uniforms, a signal of respect for a man who had served his country all his life. Others—also Navy men—came in civilian clothes, perhaps a quiet disapproval of the way the admiral had left the world.

The casket arrived through a side door, rolled in by enlisted men who positioned it in front of the altar and pulpit. A few flower arrangements flanked it. When the men finished, they took positions by the front doors, standing in a double column at parade rest.

Then they snapped to attention.

A door opened near the front, and a regal-looking woman entered, accompanied by several formally dressed younger people. Meade had never met the admiral's wife, but there was no doubt this was her—and these were the closest mourners. They stood facing the casket, backs to the congregation. The sanctuary stilled. Then they turned and took their seats in the front pew. Conversation resumed quietly as people moved forward to greet the family.

Mrs. Radford—Mary Mae—rose to greet them. From his vantage point, Meade got a clear view of her. She appeared to be in her fifties, still graceful, her beauty not diminished by time. She smiled occasionally at those who approached, receiving condolences with poise and warmth. Her dress was simple and elegant, modest yet flattering.

Lucinda had told him plenty about Mary Mae Radford. She was a fixture in Washington's high society, born into an old and influential family. Widowed young, she'd spent years as one of the city's most eligible women. Lucinda had relayed the rumors with relish.

No one quite understood why she'd married Ezra Radford, who at the time wasn't even an admiral.

Maybe it was the mystery, Lucinda had said. *Maybe he could describe what it's like to ride the waves.*

Whatever the reason, their marriage had appeared solid—despite persistent whispers of extramarital affairs on both sides. Lucinda, naturally, seemed to know every detail.

Meade studied Mary Mae. If any of the naval officers present had once been more than a friend, it wasn't obvious. She was dignified, correct, mournful, and gracious. If anyone else noticed something beneath the surface, they gave no sign.

The sanctuary was filling now. More uniforms. More civilians. Meade scanned the arriving women—wondering whether any of them might have been among the admiral's rumored liaisons. Nothing stood out.

Then he noticed a man across the sanctuary watching him.

Short and stocky, the man had the bearing of a naval officer, though he wore civilian clothes. His gaze was direct—curious, not hostile. Meade nodded. The man nodded back.

We're going to meet, Meade thought. *It's only a matter of time.*

He turned to scan the back of the sanctuary. A small group stood near the doors, less formally dressed than the seated mourners. Among them were several Black attendees—likely butlers, maids, gardeners, and janitors who had served the admiral in some capacity and felt compelled to say goodbye.

Meade had learned that Admiral Radford had been a strong advocate for opening naval ranks to African Americans after emancipation. Opposition to the idea had been fierce—sometimes violent. But the admiral had stood his ground and made progress.

Meade's eyes settled on one man in particular. Tall and older, dressed in a fine brown suit with a vest and watch chain, he had the bearing of a minister—the face of someone who had seen much of life.

That man is probably worth an interview, Meade thought.

The organ began to play softly. Conversation ebbed. Meade turned forward again, scanning the pews one last time. Then something made him turn around again.

That's when he saw her.

A young woman sat alone in the very back row. Small-framed, her face and shoulders partly hidden by long dark hair. A white handkerchief stood out against her black hooded cape. She was silently sobbing, shoulders trembling, her face buried in the handkerchief. She made no sound, drew no attention—and no one else in the congregation seemed to notice her grief.

Meade couldn't look away. Of all those present, she was the only one visibly overwhelmed by sorrow. When he finally turned back toward the pulpit, her image stayed with him.

Who is she? Why is she here, grieving like this?

She had a connection to the admiral—one I need to understand.

The organ swelled. Conversations ceased. The minister appeared from the chancel in black robes and stepped to the pulpit. The service was beginning.

Just as he opened the large Bible on the pulpit, a sound came from the back of the church. The door opened.

A tall, older man stood there—his face full of whiskers, his bearing unmistakable.

It was Hubert Meadows—Meade's father.

11: The Eulogy

EADE'S ANGER SPIKED THE moment Hubert made his grand entrance. *What the hell is he doing here?*

But that was how Hubert operated. He never let anyone know what he was doing or when he was going to do it—unless he had a motive, something to gain. Years of experience had taught Meade to always be suspicious of what Hubert was up to.

Hubert made no attempt to be quiet or avoid interrupting the proceedings. His heavy footsteps echoed throughout the sanctuary. He paused at the back and looked around; his eyes quickly landed on Meade. For the two seconds their eyes met, Hubert smiled—but it brought Meade no comfort.

Then Hubert turned, walked toward the small group of Negroes at the rear of the sanctuary, and approached the tall, well-dressed man Meade had noticed earlier. Hubert shook his hand, placed an arm around his shoulders, and spoke briefly. Despite his anger, Meade would've given anything to know what was said in that moment.

Without further delay, Hubert circled around to Meade's side of the sanctuary and made his way down to the pew. He said nothing—just climbed over Meade with his long legs and sat down beside him as if nothing were out of the ordinary.

By then, the congregation had risen to hear the invocation and sing the first hymn of the service. As the organist began the introduction to *"Jesus, Lover of My Soul,"* Meade hissed under his breath, "What the hell are you doing here?"

Hubert turned to him, met his eyes calmly. "I knew the admiral," he said. "He was a good friend." Then he opened his hymnal and began to sing—a clear signal that the conversation would wait. Meade took a deep breath and, like clockwork, found himself saying, silently, *Yes, Papa.*

Jesus, Lover of my soul,
Let me to Thy bosom fly,
While the nearer waters roll,
While the tempest still is high.
Hide me, O my Savior, hide,
Till the storm of life is past;
Safe into the haven guide,
Oh, receive my soul at last.

Sometime before the final verse, Meade forced down his frustration using his usual mind games, redirecting his thoughts to the funeral and the people in attendance.

The crowd was much larger than expected. Meade recognized several naval officers and a number of Washington's social and political elites. But many faces were unfamiliar—and that was what made the crowd interesting.

The service followed the familiar pattern: prayers, scripture readings, a brief recounting of the admiral's life, and eulogies from two fellow officers. The congregation sang each hymn with enthusiasm—Hubert especially so. When the minister stood again to announce a third and final eulogy, Meade felt it in his gut: *This is why*

Hubert is here. He was never content to simply attend—Hubert had to be *part* of the show.

But when the minister spoke, the name took Meade—and the entire congregation—by surprise.

"Professor Sylvester Watkins."

The well-dressed Negro to whom Hubert had spoken now stepped into the aisle and walked, without hesitation, toward the pulpit.

Around the sanctuary, murmurs broke out. A dozen or more people stood up and made for the exits, their footsteps loud, their departure unmistakable.

Watkins ignored them.

He climbed to the pulpit with quiet dignity, paused for effect, and commanded the room.

Meade glanced sideways. Hubert sat with arms folded, utterly relaxed, a grin flickering across his face.

Papa knows something, Meade thought. *Damn it—of course he knows something.*

"Good afternoon," Watkins said. "My name is Sylvester Watkins."

His deep, resonant voice bounced through the sanctuary's high rafters and plain walls. His posture was perfectly upright, his presence magnetic. His hair was mostly black, touched with gray, his long sideburns tapering to sharp points down his cheeks.

He reached into his coat, retrieved a folded sheet of paper, and laid it flat on the pulpit. Then he put on a pair of reading glasses.

"It is a sad honor for me to stand here today to speak about Ezra Radford. He was my shipmate. He was my colleague. In these past few years, we worked together on things that would make the

American Navy stronger. We were partners. But most of all—he was my friend."

The church was silent.

Partners, Meade thought. *That doesn't sound like suicide.*

Watkins's tone shifted—less formal, more conversational—as he told his story.

He had grown up in Philadelphia, the son of a formerly enslaved woman and a freedman father who owned a small shoe repair shop. His parents attended Mother Bethel African Methodist Episcopal Church, and every Sunday, so did he—squirming beside them in the pew.

"My father wanted me to take up the family trade," Watkins said, "but I had other ideas."

He spoke of the Navy men who would occasionally attend church—Negro sailors with weathered faces and sea stories that captured his young imagination.

"So when I was about twelve, I counted myself big enough to join up. I marched down to the harbor, boarded a U.S. Navy ship, and told the first man I saw that I wanted in. He laughed—and then he picked me up and threw me overboard."

The audience erupted with laughter, and Watkins grinned.

"That would've been the end of my naval career—and quite possibly the end of Sylvester Watkins—if it hadn't been for a young lieutenant who'd seen what happened. He dove in after me, swam down through the murk, and hauled me up like a sack of flour. That man's name was Ezra Radford."

He paused, the admiral's name catching in his throat.

Then, another grin.

"The first thing Ezra did after pulling me out was give me a nickname. From then on, I was known to him—and to everyone else—as 'Stone.' He said that's the way I swam. Like a stone."

More laughter, warmer this time.

Watkins went on to describe the admiral's mentorship.

"I could read words, but not the sea. I didn't know north from south, longitude from latitude, the depth of the ocean, or the height of a mast. Ezra Radford taught me everything. Not just how to *read* a chart—but how to *make* one."

He spoke of their time aboard the USS *Kearsarge*, of the battle against the *CSS Alabama* in Cherbourg Harbor, of Radford's leadership in the thick of war.

"Ezra Radford was the best seaman on the ship that day. In my opinion, the best man in the entire crew."

He paused again, his tone softening.

"He stayed in the Navy after the war, when so many others left. He believed in it—believed in building it up, strengthening it, even when that wasn't a popular view in this city."

Then Watkins folded his notes.

"It's time to say goodbye to our friend," he said. "It's time to offer Ezra Radford the time-honored farewell: *May you have fair winds and a following seas.*"

He stepped down from the pulpit, and the only sound in the sanctuary was the echo of his footsteps on the wooden floor.

12: Hubert Meadows

I FEAR NO FOE, with Thee at hand to bless
Ills have no weight, and tears no bitterness
Where is death's sting? Where, grave, thy victory?
I triumph still, if Thou abide with me.

As the last notes of the third verse of *"Abide With Me,"* the service's final hymn, echoed through the sanctuary, Meade subtly positioned himself to turn and look toward the back of the church. In his reporter's mind, he was trying to gauge several things—among them, how many people had already left. His major purpose, however, was to find the woman he had seen earlier—the one who was crying silently but obviously. That place in her pew was empty.

He looked toward the back doors, which had been opened by the church's ushers, and he thought he saw the final wisp of a black robe moving through the vestibule and toward the outside doors. He turned fully so he could get a good view of the back of the church. She was not there. *She can't be far away,* he thought.

With the hymn still echoing around the sanctuary, Meade put his hymnal down onto the pew, grabbed his reporter's notebook and pen, stepped out into the side aisle, and headed for the back of the church. He heard his father call after him in a loud whisper, "Meade, Meade," but he ignored those pleas. *Not responding to Hubert's com-*

mands was an event in life that gave him some satisfaction.

But Meade was not thinking about Hubert. Most of his mind and attention were centered on the woman—a person he did not know and did not recognize—but she was someone he was sure knew something about the admiral, and all of his instincts told him that she must be found.

When Meade stepped outside the church, he was confronted with the noise and clatter of a busy afternoon on New York Avenue. People crowded the sidewalks and crossed the streets in random fashion. Carriages drawn by their horses made only slight efforts to avoid the crossing pedestrians. Meade looked around, examining individuals who might resemble the woman and moving on quickly when they were rejected. All he knew about her was a vague notion of what she looked like and the black hooded cape that she wore.

Standing at the top of the church steps for several minutes, Meade had a view of at least a block and a half of New York Avenue. He thought he caught a glimpse of a black-robed woman walking up the avenue, just disappearing from view, but he could not be certain—black, after all, was the standard color that men and women wore that day, and the front of the church and beyond was beginning to be populated by the funeral mourners, most of whom were also dressed in black.

Meade decided that he should at least try to follow the black-robed woman that he thought he might have seen. He started down the steps when a strong hand grabbed his upper arm and arrested his movement.

"Where do you think you're going?" It was Hubert.

Should I offer an explanation? Meade thought. *He certainly doesn't deserve one.*

Hubert wasn't interested in Meade's explanations; instead, he commanded, "You need to come back in here with me." He had never let go of Meade's arm, and Meade knew that to free himself would result in a physical altercation that might be witnessed by dozens of people. Hubert knew the same thing.

Once inside the church, Hubert, who still had a grip on Meade's arm, maneuvered him toward a corner of the vestibule, away from the eyes and ears of any of the funeral's congregation who might be lingering there.

"The admiral's widow wants to see us," Hubert said in a low tone, but loud enough for Meade to understand that he believed this was important.

"Mary Mae Radford?"

Hubert nodded.

"Here?"

Hubert shook his head. "She wants us to come to her house."

"I suppose that means now?"

Hubert nodded again. "As soon as we can get there," he said. "I've got the carriage outside. She lives up on Massachusetts Avenue."

The fact that Hubert had "the carriage" meant that he had been to Lucinda and Meade's house on Connecticut Avenue and had commandeered their carriage as well as their horse and driver. *It also meant that Lucinda knew he was in town. He must've just arrived there, said hello, and absconded with the carriage,* Meade thought, *otherwise Lucinda would have attempted to get word to me.*

Five minutes later, Meade found himself sitting opposite Hubert in a carriage as it traveled through the heavy traffic of Washington's midday streets. Hubert peered through the openings of the carriage at the shops, pedestrians, and the general street activity. The carriage headed northeast on New York Avenue, rumbling steadily around pedestrians and other carriages. Meade observed a wide variety of Washington's working-class population, busy with their daily business. There were men, women, and children of all colors, shapes, and sizes, and even a variety of languages spoken by immigrants who had landed in Washington in search of family and work.

Washington was one of those places where you could find just about anything and do the thing you were seeking to do, where honest work and dishonest tussles lived happily side by side. Meade looked directly at Hubert.

"OK, tell me what you are doing here." Meade's voice was firm and unwavering, his eyes locked on Hubert as they returned to the inside of the carriage.

"The admiral was my friend," Hubert said. "I've known him for many years. I needed to come to his funeral."

Meade immediately recognized what he and Lucinda had come to call a *Hubert truth*—a statement that was true in itself but wasn't the whole truth. In fact, it was specifically designed to obscure the whole truth, and maybe the real truth.

"It's more than just that," Meade said flatly.

"Why do you say that?"

"Because it's always more than just that with you. That's the way you operate. Now I suggest you level with me, or I'll stop the carriage, get out, and walk away."

"That's not going to happen," Hubert muttered and took a deep breath.

Low-slung shabby houses and shops with hand-painted signs occupied most of New York Avenue at street level. As they approached Mount Vernon Square, the street population had cleared to some degree, and the carriage was making better time. Meade still had a lot of questions for Hubert.

"How do you know Sylvester Watkins?" Meade asked.

Hubert, who had been looking out the other side of the carriage, registered some surprise at the question.

"Who says I knew him?" His tone was gruff; he did not want to broach the subject, but Meade was not going to let it go.

"I saw you talking to him before the service began."

Hubert conceded the point. "The admiral introduced me to him some years ago. Sylvester Watkins is one of the smartest people I've ever met. He is teaching at Howard University now, but he can't get a professorship." Hubert chuckled somewhat bitterly. "That's a Black university, and the only people who can get professorships are white men."

Hubert fell silent for a moment.

Then he continued, "I have been trying to get Watkins to leave this place and move to Nashville to start teaching at Fisk. He's as stubborn as a mule, though; he won't leave Washington."

Another of Hubert's subterfuges, Meade thought.

At Mount Vernon Square, the carriage made a left turn onto Massachusetts Avenue and headed toward the northwest. The environment of the street was suddenly different; the homes along that street were large and elegant, and they grew larger and more elaborate as the carriage made its way up the avenue.

Hubert was a tall man with a large round head. His receding hairline was obscured by a massive amount of facial hair, the generosity of which often distracted listeners. Hubert was dressed in a plain brown suit, and from his waistcoat hung a bright gold watch chain—the only sign of his prosperity.

Hubert was not a vain man, Meade thought. *For that much I can give him credit.* Meade even considered congratulating himself on his generosity toward his father, but he remembered his anger at seeing him at the church, and now he was interested to hear what Hubert had to say for himself.

"Why are we going to Mary Mae Radford's house?"

Meade was determined to get as much information out of Hubert as he could. Hubert was being his stingy self in that regard, but the carriage left Hubert with no exit options; he had to sit there and at least hear the questions.

"Mary Mae is an old friend," Hubert said. "I have known her for years, long before she met and married the admiral. When she saw that I was at the service, well, that's when she invited us to her house."

Something had changed in Hubert's tone as he talked about Mary Mae Radford, and Meade made a mental note: *Just what was the relationship? Was it more than friendship? This would be one of the topics of discussion he would have with Lucinda as soon as he could.*

Hubert was a widower; his wife had died soon after their younger sister Caroline had been born. As far as the children knew, Hubert had never had another romance, but they also knew that Hubert had his secrets.

"She specifically asked that you come with me," Hubert said.

"Why me?"

"She had seen you in the sanctuary before the service began. She said she wanted to talk to you."

"Do you know why?"

Hubert gave a light shrug. "I'll let her say what she has to say."

Meade stared hard at Hubert, and Hubert must have felt the stare.

"Listen, son. I know that you've been poking around the Navy and other places asking about the admiral's death." *Just like Hubert,* Meade thought. *He knows everyone and everything, and even when he's more than 500 miles away in Nashville, he still knows what I am up to.* "I'm not going to tell you to stop your investigation," Hubert said. "I don't think the admiral committed suicide; in fact, I'm sure he didn't. I have known him for decades; he wouldn't do that."

"You're not the only one who believes that."

"I know that too. But I also know there are people who want everybody else to believe it—or at least people who would rather not have any inconvenient truth come to light. What I am telling you is that if you persist in this, you could well be putting yourself in danger."

Again, Meade looked straight at Hubert. "Do you think that's something I can't handle?"

"No, I think you can," Hubert said. "I just want to make sure that you're prepared for it."

Meade knew that Hubert did not use the word *danger* lightly. Hubert didn't use any word lightly, and he certainly knew what danger was.

He had faced plenty of danger in his hometown of Nashville, where, before the Civil War began, Hubert was one of the few outspoken Unionists to reside. The town was steeped in secessionist fever, but Hubert never bothered to curb his beliefs or temper his words. He made enemies—some of whom, given the chance, would have killed him.

In 1861, his lumber business suffered because of those political views. But by 1862, Hubert had gotten lucky—a turn of events that seemed to be a recurring theme in his life. Union forces under

Ulysses Grant occupied Nashville, relieving Hubert of the imminent danger of being jailed as a traitor or lynched outright.

From that point forward, Hubert remained personally at risk, but he no longer lacked for customers. The United States government and its army—eventually under the command of William Tecumseh Sherman—were the only clients he really needed.

When Sherman took command, his goal was to drive his army down through Chattanooga into Atlanta and through the heart of the Confederacy. To do that, he needed timber—rail ties, bridge planks, fortifications, everything. That meant Hubert got very rich, very fast.

But the danger never went away.

Meade, who was ten years old when the war ended, remembered that danger keenly. Hubert's lumber business sat on Main Street, on the east side of the Cumberland River, and throughout the war, Hubert had fortified it—hiring men he trusted and arming them well. Despite the Union army's presence, secessionist sentiment still ran hot in Nashville. The army was not a police force. Hubert had to provide his own security.

Meade could tell many stories—too many—about the dangers they faced and the close calls they barely escaped. Lucinda, two years younger, had trouble understanding what was happening at the time, but even she came to know that the world outside their enclave was not a safe place.

When Hubert talks about danger, Meade thought, *he knows exactly what he's talking about.*

He stewed on his father's words, caught in a familiar mix of exasperation, anger, and reluctant respect. He knew Hubert better than anyone—but there were times when he felt he didn't know him at all. Hubert never hesitated to share his opinions, but the people he knew and the things he did were often kept carefully hidden.

And so, Meade was sure: Hubert hadn't come to Washington *just* to attend the admiral's funeral. There was something larger at play, and somehow, Meade had gotten himself caught up in it—a game of events in which Hubert was already a piece on the board.

Meade had questions. Many questions. He doubted Hubert would answer them. And yet, even that line of thought gave way to another.

At the top of his mind now was the woman from the funeral. Who was she? Why had her grief been so raw, so visible, while everyone else remained composed? What had she known about the admiral—and why had she slipped away so quickly and quietly?

She's gone, Meade thought. *I may have lost any chance of finding her.*

He had only a vague memory of her appearance. And in a city like Washington, there must be hundreds of women who matched that description. Still, he clung to the hope that if she had information—real, important information—she would find her way back to the story somehow.

Across from him, Hubert sat adjusting his tie and vest—small details, but Meade noticed. They weren't the kind of movements he usually saw from his father. *Was he preparing himself to see Mary Mae Radford?*

But before Meade could return to the questions he wanted to hurl at his father, the carriage slowed, then stopped.

"We're here," Hubert said, and climbed out.

Meade followed.

13: Nathan Tower

AT THE SAME TIME that Hubert and Meade were heading northwest on Massachusetts Avenue, Commander Nathan Tower was taking a more secure route in the opposite direction. He was on foot and walked straight from the New York Avenue Presbyterian Church to his destination. The journey might have taken 20 minutes, but on this particular afternoon, Tower calculated that it would take at least twice that long.

The funeral service for the admiral had lasted longer than he'd hoped. Sylvester Watkins, he conceded, was a compelling speaker—but he talked too long and, in Tower's estimation, said too much.

Tower prided himself on being unremarkable—blending in was part of the job. His build was stocky, his features average, and though he kept a full head of hair well into his sixties, he trimmed it short enough to avoid notice. He wore civilian clothes and could blend into nearly any crowd.

He zigzagged his way to Pennsylvania Avenue, walked southeast toward the Capitol for two blocks, then cut back north. In the midst of pedestrian traffic, he stepped into a recessed doorway and lingered for half a minute, waiting for the street to crowd up again. He crossed quickly, dodged a carriage, then looped back toward

Pennsylvania Avenue.

A passing electric streetcar offered cover; Tower hopped aboard, rode two blocks, then stepped off near a dense crowd. He mingled easily. A block later, he stopped in front of a store window, pretending to inspect the display. The reflection showed a regular flow of foot traffic—no one loitering, no obvious tails.

Tower resumed his route. He ducked into the Washington Hotel at Pennsylvania and Third, cut through the lobby, and exited the side door, where he hailed a carriage-for-hire. It dropped him off in front of the Capitol. From there, he continued west on Maine Avenue, eyes flicking to passing faces. Again, nothing.

He turned down Virginia Avenue toward the Navy Yard but veered north on Fourth Street before reaching the water. The street was deserted—perfect.

After several blocks, he reached a three-story, aging brick house with a simple sign reading: **Boarding House.** A notice beneath it: **No Vacancies.**

This was Tower's house—not his by deed or rent, but by control.

The porch bore two unused rocking chairs. Three men lived in the first-floor rooms, including Burley O'Malley. All had been instructed to say the house was full—though the upper floors remained empty.

Tower entered and paused at the bottom of the stairs. "Burley," he called.

"Up here, Captain," came the response.

Tower climbed to the second floor and turned left into a spacious, sparse room. Burley O'Malley sat at a table, a half-empty glass of beer in his hand. A full one waited beside it.

"How was the funeral?" Burley asked.

Tower took a long drink. The dodging had left him parched. "Sad, but too long."

Burley nodded solemnly, then raised his glass. "To the old man."

"To the old man," Tower echoed, voice edged with respect. "He didn't deserve to go the way he did."

They drank in silence, reflective.

"What's next?" Burley asked eventually.

"What's next is figuring out what we're up against."

"You got any ideas?"

"Oh yeah," Tower said. "Plenty. First, the admiral was murdered. The question isn't just how or who—but why."

He glanced at Burley, who seemed to be studying his drink. Tower's mind wandered—to Berlin, a decade ago, when he served as naval attaché. There he met Wilhelm Stieber, Bismarck's spymaster. Stieber had taken a liking to the American, shared his methods over several clandestine meetings.

If you are going to get into this business, Stieber had said, *you must have some feet on the ground. Someone hard as German steel. Someone you can trust with anything. And you'll be lucky to find even one.*

Tower looked at Burley and felt himself fortunate.

Burley caught Tower's thoughtful look. "What's got you bugged up, boss?"

"Trying to get a handle on this. The Navy's been modernizing—fast. And we're doing a pretty damn good job."

Burley nodded.

"The problem with doing a good job," Tower continued, "is that people start noticing. And if they're noticing, they're not just watching—they're acting."

"They're trying to get inside the mess hall, huh, boss?"

Tower paused. "Not just inside, Burley. They're trying to steal the food."

"And our job is to figure out who the thieves are—and what they're after."

"I have an idea about both." Tower leaned in. "The Navy has a clandestine team in Spain, surveying the coastline. Officially, they're four students from Howard University, on a language and culture tour."

"And they're sending back intel," Burley said.

"Exactly. When it's done, we'll have the most accurate navigational data on Spain's defenses in the world. Top-secret work. Especially the maps. Those maps are gold. Every major nation would kill to get them."

"Including Spain."

"Especially Spain."

Burley let that settle in.

"And the admiral was in charge of all that."

Tower gave a grim smile. "Didn't take you long to make that leap."

Burley took a last sip, not acknowledging the compliment. "So if the admiral was murdered, someone knows about the project—someone who shouldn't."

He stood and left. Tower assumed he'd gone for a refill.

Tower's mind returned to Berlin. *We are in a giant chess game, my boy,* Stieber had told him. *One that will last beyond our lifetimes. You don't win or lose—you just keep playing.*

Ständiger Krieg. Constant war. Espionage never ceased. The illusion of peace was just that—an illusion.

Burley returned with a pitcher and filled their glasses.

"So, boss—what's the plan?"

"I'm pretty sure Spain's behind this. But they can't act directly. Too risky. They've bought someone—someone they don't think we'll recognize."

"Who?"

"I don't know. But we've got to find out. There's a lot riding on this."

"Meade Meadows," Burley said. "You think he's part of this? He's been nosing around. And he was nearby when the admiral died."

Tower considered. "Meade Meadows isn't working for Spain. I've watched him a while. Known his father for years. In fact, his father is part of what we're doing. He's one of the few Americans who understands that we have enemies and that we need to know what they're up to. No—Meade's a solid reporter. Honest."

Burley nodded.

"But is he part of all this?" Tower added. "Yes. He may be the key—even if he doesn't realize it."

They lapsed into silence again. Tower brooded while Burley turned something over in his mind.

"Don't make no sense, Cap'n."

Tower looked up. "What's that?"

Burley searched for the words. "Well, the war's been over twenty years. You'd think folks were over it."

"Some people have very long memories," Tower said with a sigh.

"I ain't talking about memories."

"What are you talking about?"

"I've been hearing stuff. Things I ain't never heard before. There's Rebs still mad 'cause we beat 'em. But this ain't from them. It's from younger folks. Some of 'em weren't even born till after the war."

Tower leaned forward. "A new generation? Young Confederates—angry about what happened to their parents?"

Burley nodded. "Yeah. That's what I'm talking about."

Tower absorbed it. "Keep your ears open. Let me know what you hear." Then another thought struck him. "Listen, Burley. I want you to do a little more than that."

14: Mary Mae Radford

THE FRESHLY PAINTED HOUSE where Ezra and Mary Mae Radford resided sat on a small, neatly trimmed lawn just a few feet away from Massachusetts Avenue. The house and all its trimmings spoke of generational wealth.

Hubert bounded out of the carriage, hit the ground walking without missing a step, and didn't glance back as he made his way to the front of the house. Meade scrambled down from the carriage and hurried to catch up. By the time he reached the front, Meade was pressing the doorbell.

Only seconds later, the door was opened by a young, petite, pleasant-looking woman whom Meade estimated to be about 20 years old. She was dressed in the neatly pressed garments of a housemaid.

"Good afternoon, Mr. Meadows," she said, her eyes brightening somewhat when she recognized the old man standing in front of her.

"Good afternoon, Julia," Hubert replied.

Meade detected a slight curtsey but noted her manner was direct and American.

"Miss Radford will be down in a few minutes," Julia said, stepping aside from the door so they could enter. "She is in the drawing room. We're making some tea right now."

Once inside, Julia closed the front door, turned, and looked at

Meade.

"This is my son, Meade," Hubert said.

Again, there was a slight curtsey. "Pleased to meet you, sir."

"And you too, Julia," Meade said.

Without any direction, Hubert headed to his left into a spacious and fashionably furnished room with a large fireplace.

Meade was astonished. He had no idea that Hubert had ever been in this house. Hubert had certainly not mentioned anything about being here during his visits to Washington.

When he thought they were outside the hearing of the house-maid, he turned to Hubert and said, "You know this place? You've been here?"

"Many times," Hubert replied.

"You've never said anything about knowing these people well enough to have been in their home," Meade said, trying to talk quietly, but his voice was intense.

"I know lots of people," Hubert said. "I've been to lots of places." With that, and only that, he took a seat in a large chair next to the fireplace.

Once again, Meade thought, *Hubert knows far more than he ever lets on.*

The large room absorbed the heavy silence between them. Meade took a moment to gather himself and let his reporter's instincts kick in. He looked around the room. The large windows on two sides let in ample afternoon sun. The room wasn't overcrowded with furniture. On the walls hung portraits—likely past generations of those who had occupied the house. Artistically, the portraits weren't very good, but they made a statement: this was a room where much had happened.

As Meade was taking all of this in, Julia entered with a large tea tray full of cups, saucers, a teapot, utensils, and small portions of elegantly cut cake. She set the tray down on a table in front of the fireplace, poured a cup of tea, and said, "I believe you take yours with milk, don't you, Mr. Meadows?"

Turning to Meade: "And how would you like your tea, sir?"

Meade said that he preferred it without anything in it.

"Very good, sir," she said, handing it to him.

"Thank you, Julia," came a voice from the doorway. It was Mary Mae Radford. "That will be all for now," she said to the maid. "Please close the door and make sure that we are not disturbed."

Julia curtsied—visibly this time. "Very good, madame," she said, and left the room.

As Julia closed the double doors, Mary Mae Radford walked directly over to Hubert, put her arms around him, and kissed him on the cheek. "Thank you, Hubert," she said. "Thank you for coming today. Ezra would've been glad to see you."

Meade noticed that Hubert had not been shy about putting his arms around the admiral's widow; he seemed to hold her a beat too long—closer than friendship required.

"Mary," he said, "I would not have been anywhere but here today. You know that."

"I know that, Hubert," she said quietly. Her voice and face were full of emotion. After a few moments of silence, she hugged him again—and to Meade's eyes, he held her tightly.

She then stepped away and turned to Meade. "Now, introduce me to your very handsome son."

Without waiting for Hubert, Meade extended his hand. "Good afternoon, Mrs. Radford. I'm Meade Meadows. I am very sorry about the admiral's death."

"Thank you, Meade, and thank you for coming to the funeral to-day." She had recovered her proper-hostess voice. She looked around and said, "Gentlemen, please be seated. I see Julia has given you tea. Can I offer anything else?"

Hubert and Meade both shook their heads.

Mary Mae poured herself a cup and sat on a sofa facing them. Meade had been impressed by her at the church; seeing her up close confirmed it. She must have been a strikingly beautiful young woman, and much of that beauty remained. She also radiated control. Her smile was warm, but it conveyed intelligence more than intimacy. Despite her grief, she carried herself with grace.

She had changed from her black mourning dress to a dark blue frock—appropriate, but not festive.

She took a sip and looked directly at Meade. "I want to thank you also for coming with your father today. I understand that you've been asking about the admiral's death. That is something I want to talk to you about."

Meade shot an accusatory look at Hubert. Mary Mae saw it and shook her head.

"Hubert hasn't told me anything," she said. "I have my own sources."

Meade straightened. "Just what have you heard?"

"Despite what your newspaper has written," she said, "I have a feeling that you don't believe my husband committed suicide. If that's true, I want to tell you that you are right—Ezra did not kill himself."

"Why do you say that, Mrs. Radford?"

"I have many reasons. He was my husband. I knew him better

than anyone. He wasn't depressed. In fact, he told me this was the most important work of his career."

"What work was that?"

She looked at Hubert, who said nothing.

"I don't know. He wouldn't talk about it—not with me or anyone I knew."

"Was that unusual?"

"Yes," she replied. "He used to talk about everything he did. The Navy was his favorite subject. Ask Hubert."

Both looked at Hubert, who only smiled.

"When did he stop sharing details?"

"I'm not sure—maybe nine months ago. I thought he was just bored. But when I asked, he said it was important work he couldn't talk about. Not even with me."

"You think he didn't trust you?"

"No, I think he was trying to protect me. *From something real. Something dangerous.*"

The three sat quietly with her words. "You see, Meade, the Navy is changing. We're entering a new era. It's a dangerous time. Most Americans think we're removed from it—but those oceans between us and Europe and Asia aren't as big as they used to be."

She refilled her cup and offered more to Hubert and Meade. Hubert accepted. Meade declined.

"Was the admiral working with Sylvester Watkins?"

Mary Mae took a breath. "Yes. I don't know the details. But they'd known each other for years. As you heard, they were shipmates during the war."

"Why didn't Watkins stay in the Navy?"

"Ezra wanted him to, but there wasn't space for him after the war.

The Navy was shrinking, and some pushed hard to get Negroes to resign. Most did."

"How did Ezra feel?"

"Disappointed. He thought the Navy was losing good people. But he also knew Sylvester was destined for more than being a seaman or a manservant."

"Was Ezra pushing the Navy to re-accept Negroes?"

She nodded. "It was something he really believed in."

"Do you think he pushed too hard?"

"I don't know. It's possible. *You know how people are.*"

"Is that what got him killed?"

She didn't flinch. "The thought has crossed my mind."

Hubert joined in. "It's a big issue with some people—bigger than you'd believe."

"Big enough to get him killed?" Meade asked.

Hubert shook his head. "I don't see anyone in the Navy committing murder over it."

"What about someone outside the Navy?"

"Possible. There are people who don't want any race mixing. Still…"

He trailed off. Mary Mae picked up the thread. "There's another rumor going around: that the admiral became so secretive, he might've been planning treachery."

"Treachery?" Meade echoed.

"That he might've planned to betray his country."

That's not the first time I've heard that, Meade thought. *Quiet talk. Nothing solid—but enough to be troubling.*

"That's why I asked you here. Ezra Radford was no traitor. He loved this country."

"I can vouch for that," Hubert said.

Mary Mae continued, "I know we can't bring him back. But if you could find out why he was killed, maybe you could stop people from calling him a traitor."

Meade nodded. He already believed Ezra hadn't taken his own life. "I will do my best."

The conversation seemed done, but Meade had one more question.

"I'll need your help."

"Certainly," she said.

"Did the admiral do much work in this house?"

"He had a study upstairs."

"I'd like to take a look."

15: The Admiral's Study

Heavy, dark drapes blocked the afternoon sun from illuminating any part of the large room on the third floor of Mary Mae Radford's house—the room that had been designated as the admiral's study. Meade entered alone, and the memory of what he had seen in the admiral's office flashed through his mind.

His presence in that office remained a closely guarded secret, known only to him, Lucinda, and whoever had been in the hallway the night of the end—the person Meade was certain was the admiral's killer.

He hadn't expected Mary Mae to grant him access to the study so readily or openly. When she did, Meade asked if she wanted to accompany him.

"I'm sorry," she had said. "I just don't think it would do me much good to go into that room right now."

He said he understood and suggested she might help if anything needed to be unlocked.

"I'll send Julia up in a few minutes," she said. "She'll stay in the hallway, but if you need anything, she can probably provide it. Meanwhile, I'd rather stay here and have a conversation with your father."

Meade glanced at Hubert and caught a look of satisfaction on his face.

"Meade's a pretty good reporter and investigator," Hubert said to Mary Mae. "If there's something up there worth finding, he'll probably find it."

It was typical Hubert—praise that might or might not be sincere, but Meade appreciated it nonetheless.

The study was larger than Meade expected. Light from the hallway let him find the drapes facing Massachusetts Avenue. When he opened them, sunlight spilled across the room. He crossed to the side wall and opened those drapes as well. The room came into full view.

It smelled of tobacco and old books. One wall was lined with bookshelves filled with volumes on navigation, naval history, Shakespeare, and popular novels. One book stood apart: *Adventures of Tom Sawyer*. Meade took it down. On the frontispiece was Mark Twain's signature.

Maritime paintings and prints hung on the walls. One photo—a Matthew Brady portrait of Abraham Lincoln, beardless and poised for the presidency—had Lincoln's signature beneath it. Meade imagined the pride the admiral must have felt owning it.

A soft knock pulled Meade from his thoughts. Julia stood in the doorway.

"Excuse me, sir," she said. "Mrs. Radford wanted me to give you this key."

Meade took a good look at her for the first time. Likely between eighteen and twenty, she was petite and composed. Her confidence struck him even more than her height—barely five feet, if that.

She stepped in and placed a small key on the admiral's desk, then turned to leave.

"Do you know what the key is for?" Meade asked.

"No, sir," she said. She paused, thinking. "I've cleaned this room top to bottom. There's nothing I know of that's locked."

"None of the drawers?"

"No, sir."

"No wall safes or hidden compartments?"

"Not that I've seen."

She waited, still, as if sensing he might ask more.

"Thank you, Julia. That's very helpful."

"Yes, sir." Julia hesitated for a moment, but Meade had already turned back toward the room. He was concentrating on the key. She watched him carefully for as long as she could. Then she shut the door to the study.

Meade turned the key over in his hand several times, trying his best to see what the key might tell him. It was small—too small to fit anything large. It looked familiar, but he couldn't place it. *It'll come to me,* he told himself.

He laid the key on the desk. Finding what it opened was now his mission. He began searching behind the pictures on the wall.

He started with the Lincoln photo. Behind it: nothing. He pried at the backing of the frame with his penknife. Still nothing. He carefully reassembled and rehung it.

He repeated the process with the rest. A few odd items surfaced, but nothing related to the admiral's recent work.

Next: the bookshelves. He used a ladder to reach the top, checking behind the volumes. No compartments. A few cracked plaster seams, nothing more.

He opened the thickest books, hoping one might be hollow. None were.

He examined the furniture—the chairs, the small sofa—feeling underneath but seeing no cause to cut the upholstery. He moved rugs and checked the floor. Again, nothing.

More than an hour had passed. The light was fading. Meade turned on the wall sconces and desk lamp. He muttered, *There's got to be something somewhere in here.*

Everything had been checked—except the admiral's desk.

He sat at it. The red oak surface was polished, orderly. Pens, a blotter, calendar, a couple of cryptic notes. No locks visible on the drawers.

The desk had a central shallow drawer and three drawers on each side. Meade opened each—left side first. Personal letters, old files. Nothing stood out. The bottom drawer had a false bottom—he pried it up. Empty.

He moved to the right. Same story.

The desk reminded him of time spent as a teenager in Hubert's lumber company shop. A carpenter named Luther—Meade couldn't recall his last name—had taken a shine to him and shown him little woodworking tricks. "Secrets," Luther had called them.

Come on, Luther, Meade thought, *don't fail me now.*

He compared the drawer lengths—those on the right were longer than those on the left. *Interesting.*

He pulled out the center drawer, placed it on the floor, and got down on his knees.

There it was.

On the left support column, hidden behind the center drawer's frame, was a keyhole.

Meade inserted the small key and turned it. A hidden compartment swung open.

His breath caught slightly.

Inside: a small leather-bound notebook, some loose papers, a letter opener with an ornate carved handle, and a rolled-up navigational map.

He pulled everything onto the floor and spread them in the fading light. The map's details were striking—precise, meticulous. He turned the notebook in his hands and flipped it open.

What were you working on, Admiral?

As he skimmed the first few pages, a knock came at the door. Julia.

"Sir," she said, not surprised to see him on the floor, "Mrs. Radford asked me to tell you she and Mr. Meadows have gone to the Imperial Hotel for dinner. She said you're welcome to join them—or I could fix you a light supper and bring it here."

The mention of dinner made him realize he was hungry. Julia couldn't see what he had laid out.

"No, thank you, Julia. I'll decline both. I think it's time I headed home."

"Very good, sir. Anything you'd like me to tell Mrs. Radford?"

"Please thank her for her hospitality. I'll be in touch again soon."

Julia nodded and left.

Meade gathered the items, shut the hidden compartment, and locked it. He replaced the drawer, scanned the room one last time, and left.

Outside, he flagged a carriage-for-hire. He checked—carefully—that he still had everything.

So carefully, in fact, that he didn't notice Burley O'Malley, standing across the street, leaning against a tree.

The old sailor was following an order Commander Nathan Tower had given him earlier that afternoon:

Keep watch on Meade Meadows for a few days and see where he goes and what he does.

16: The Torn Map

MEADE SAT IN HIS study, staring at the items he had taken from the admiral's house. A half-eaten plate of food had been shoved to the corner of his desk. He picked up each item—the papers, the notebook, the letter opener—examining them carefully before placing them down on another part of the desk. *Was there some magic arrangement that would reveal their significance? Did these items mean anything at all?*

Meade could imagine all sorts of things, but nothing in his imagination so far made much sense. The leather notebook contained writing of various kinds; most of it was recognizable as the admiral's handwriting, but the content of the notes was varied and scattered.

Meade pushed his chair back and stared at the ceiling for a moment. Then he turned and looked out the window. *Maybe not looking at the items would be better than scrutinizing them,* he thought. *Maybe something will come to me.*

Meade had been at his house for nearly an hour. Fortunately, the cook was there, and he had been able to ask for some supper. Unfortunately, Lucinda was not there, and no one knew where she had gone or when she would be back.

When he couldn't figure something out, Lucinda was the person he relied on. He needed her now.

As if in answer to his prayers, Meade heard the door open, the unmistakable fall of her footsteps down the hallway, and, a moment later, the glorious sound of her voice. A few seconds later, the door to the study opened, and there she stood.

"What's all this?" she asked, looking at the items on Meade's desk.

"It's a very long story," Meade said.

Lucinda pulled off the gloves she had been wearing, unpinned her hat from her luxurious head of hair, and laid them on a table in the corner of the room. She then walked over and sat in a chair beside Meade.

"Tell me everything, brother," she said. "Start at the beginning."

It took Meade a moment to decide where the beginning was. While he was doing so, he asked her, "Do you want something to eat or drink?"

"I'll have some tea brought in for us."

She left the room to go into the kitchen, and while she was gone, Meade gathered his thoughts. He knew that Lucinda expected a full, detailed narrative of his day, and he was determined to remember everything he could and to tell her everything.

Lucinda returned and said, "The tea will be here in a minute. Now, start your story."

Meade looked at Lucinda. She was as fresh and beautiful as ever. Whatever she had been doing all day had not depleted her freshness or energy in any way. She was alert and attentive, seeming to hang on his every word, description, and tone.

Meade began by telling Lucinda about the admiral's funeral. It did not take him long to get to the part about their father's surprise entrance.

"Did you know he was coming?" Meade asked.

Lucinda shook her head. "The first I knew of it was when he showed up here at the house and wanted the carriage. I thought about trying to get word to you, but there simply wasn't time. He told me he was headed straight to the church."

Meade nodded with understanding. "I know how Papa is; we've seen him like that too many times."

"What else happened at the funeral?" Meade described some of the people who were there, including Sylvester Watkins. He also described the woman who seemed so grief-stricken. Lucinda was especially interested in what he said about her.

"So you did not get a good look at her face?"

Meade shook his head. "It was partially covered by the hood she was wearing, but it was obvious that she was grieving the admiral's loss—more than anyone else in the sanctuary."

"And you tried to find her as soon as the service was over?"

"I ran outside before they had even stopped singing the final hymn," Meade said. "I saw someone in a black robe retreating up New York Ave., but I'm not sure that was her. Otherwise, there was no sign at all."

"Did you see her talking with anyone or making any contact at all with anyone else at the service?"

"As far as I know, she sat by herself and didn't say anything to anyone."

"No one approached her?"

"Not that I could see."

Lucinda looked at Meade for a moment, but he knew that she was processing all of this through her analytical brain. "OK, tell me what else happened," she said.

Meade continued with what he remembered of the funeral, including the eulogy by Sylvester Watkins and the fact that there were those who walked out of the church before he began speaking.

"You said that Papa shook hands with him before the service began," Lucinda said.

"Yes, right after he came into the sanctuary."

"And he didn't greet anyone else?"

"No, Watkins was the only one. But the service had started by that time."

"That wouldn't have stopped Papa if he had wanted to say hello to anyone else."

Meade then told Lucinda about Hubert grabbing him in front of the church and putting him in the carriage for the ride to the admiral's house.

"How much did you argue with Papa during your journey?" Lucinda's tone had an accusatory ring.

"Not much," Meade mumbled.

"More than you should have, I would imagine," she said. "You know how useless that is."

Since they were children, Lucinda had heard the arguments between Meade and Hubert. Meade believed Lucinda could have recited word for word the argument they had had in the carriage if she had chosen to.

"So, once you got to the admiral's house, what happened?"

Meade talked about meeting Mary Mae. He also told Lucinda about Hubert's and Mary Mae's reactions to each other. Meade then voiced his suspicions.

"Do you think there has ever been anything going on between those two?"

Meade's question provoked a loud and sharp laugh from Lucinda.

Meade gave her a puzzled look.

"Oh, my dear naïve brother," she said, "I don't mean to laugh, but as observant as you are, sometimes you miss the very obvious."

"What do you mean by that?"

Lucinda took a breath and smiled. "I don't think there was anything between those two while she was married to the admiral. Papa and Ezra Radford were good friends, and I don't believe Papa would betray a friend. But Mary Mae Radford did not marry the admiral until after she had been widowed and single for a very long time. Do I think there was a history there between those two? I don't know, but I certainly wouldn't be surprised."

"Before I left the house this afternoon," Meade said, "I was told that Papa and Mary Mae had already gone out to dinner together."

Lucinda gave her brother a knowing look. "They are old friends," she said. "It's too soon after the admiral's death to think that anything is going to happen, but you never know what might develop." She paused for a moment. "Now, tell me what Mary Mae said to you."

Meade summarized his conversation, telling Lucinda that Mary Mae did not believe the admiral had committed suicide, and that she knew there were rumors about the admiral that were harmful to his reputation. Meade told Lucinda that Mary Mae had asked him specifically to try to find out why the admiral had been killed and to do what he could to tamp down those rumors.

"Why does she think the admiral was killed?" Lucinda asked.

"She thinks it might have to do with some project he was working on for the Navy—something that was highly secret and might have put him in danger."

"But she had no idea what this might be?"

"No," Meade said, "or at least she said she didn't."

"Do you believe her?"

"Yes," Meade said, *"but I am open to the possibility that she may not be telling everything she knows."*

"But she gave you permission to go up and search the admiral's study?"

"Yes, that's right."

"And this is what you found?" she said, looking at the items spread across the desk.

Meade was about to tell her how he had figured out where the secret compartment was in the desk when they were interrupted by the sound of the doorbell. She got up, walked out of the study, and opened the front door. Meade could hear voices. One was Lucinda's, but the other belonged to a woman he did not recognize.

In another minute, Lucinda came back into the study, accompanied by Julia, the maid at Mary Mae Radford's house.

Lucinda turned to Julia and said, "I believe you know my brother."

"Good evening, Mr. Meadows," Julia greeted.

Meade rose from his chair and said, "Good evening, Julia. I'm sorry, but no one has told me your last name."

"My name is Julia Porter," she said. "The reason I came to your house tonight was that you dropped this during your search of the admiral's study this afternoon." She thrust out her hand, which contained Meade's penknife. "You must've dropped this during your search, and I wanted to bring it straight back to you."

Meade took the penknife out of Julia's hand, noticing that Lucinda was eyeing her very carefully—more carefully than he expected. Something in her posture shifted slightly, almost imperceptibly. Lucinda was assessing this young woman, who now appeared neither as shy nor as demure as she had been earlier that afternoon.

"Thank you," he said. His words were absent any expression. Instead, he was studying Julia. *She was different now.* This was not the quiet servant who had curtsied at the admiral's front door. She held herself with more confidence, more purpose.

"Mr. Meadows, I should tell you that you did an excellent job of replacing everything that you moved in the admiral's study." She paused and looked at the penknife he was now holding. "However, you should know that the backs of all the pictures and prints on the wall have been permanently damaged."

Lucinda said nothing, but Meade saw the way she continued to study Julia—not suspiciously, but curiously. *Not what I expected from a housemaid,* her expression seemed to say.

"Fortunately, Mr. Meadows, I have a solution to this problem. I know someone who can repair the damage at a reasonable cost and with a minimum of fuss. Mrs. Radford will never know that anything is amiss. It will all be put right by tomorrow afternoon."

By this time, Meade had recovered something of his voice. He managed to stammer out, "If I agree to pay for it, correct?"

"Yes, that is the assumption I am making."

"Then I will certainly agree to that," he said emphatically. "Please have the bill sent to me, and I will include something extra in it for you."

"That is not necessary." She was not smiling when she said it.

"But I insist."

"And I insist that you do not."

Meade was stymied. *But how can I say how grateful I am to you?*

Julia relaxed her demeanor slightly. "Mr. Meadows, I appreciate what you are doing for Mrs. Radford. I am very fond of her, as I was of the admiral. I want to help you in any way I can. I thought this might be something I could do."

Julia's explanation provided Lucinda a chance to recover her voice.

"Miss Porter, how long have you worked for the Radford household?" Lucinda asked.

Julia seemed taken aback by the question. "Why, a little more than a year, I think," she replied. "Why do you ask?"

"One of the things Mrs. Radford told me was that she noticed the admiral had become more secretive about his work with the Navy in the last six months or so," Lucinda said. "Was that your observation too?"

Julia thought for a moment. "Yes, I think that's right. The admiral used to talk a lot about his work, but that trailed off probably six months ago. I noticed, too, that he would work a lot through the night."

All three were silent for a moment, considering whether this information had any importance. Then Julia spoke up.

"Mr. Meadows, I noticed that the key I had given you was not in his study, and I assume that you took it with you. Did you ever find what that key unlocked?"

Meade seemed glad for the question because he had not yet explained to Lucinda how he had discovered the locked compartment in the admiral's desk. This gave him a chance to do so—to two pretty females—and he told them how he did it with great relish.

"Miss Porter, please forgive my brother for bragging," Lucinda said.

"Oh, I didn't think he was bragging," Julia replied. "I think he is quite clever."

The beam on Meade's face was quickly cut short by Lucinda's raised eyebrow.

"Are these the things you found in the admiral's secret compartment?" Julia asked as she looked toward the top of the desk.

In for a penny, in for a pound, Meade thought. Neither he nor Lucinda had tried to conceal what was on the desk. Maybe Julia could give them some insight.

"Are any of these items anything that you have seen before?" Meade asked.

Julia walked around the desk and looked carefully at each item, careful not to touch or pick up anything. She placed her hands behind her back and leaned over the desk to examine each piece as thoroughly as possible without touching it. Lucinda concentrated on Julia's face to see if she could detect any hint of recognition toward any of the items. But more than that, she was trying to understand the girl. There was a keenness in her manner that surprised her—not inappropriate, but unusual.

Julia finally answered Meade's question. "No, I do not think that I have seen any of these things before."

Lucinda leaned slightly forward, her gaze narrowing—not out of mistrust, but interest. *She's not just a maid,* she thought. *She knows more than she says. Or at least, she wants to know more.*

Julia finally answered Meade's question. "No, I do not think that I have seen any of these things before."

Meade gave her a moment of silence to see if she had any other thoughts.

"The map is interesting, isn't it?" she said.

"How so?"

"Well, I can't say that I have seen this particular map before, but I know that the admiral was working with a set of maps," she explained. "There were several times when I entered the study to ask if he wanted something to eat or drink, and there were maps spread across his desk."

"Maps of what?" Meade asked. "Could you tell anything about the maps?"

"Oh no, I don't have any idea about that. I never got close enough to his desk to see exactly what he was working on while he was working. I rarely went any farther into the room than the doorway."

Julia looked again at the map on Meade's desk. "May I pick it up?" she asked.

"Certainly," Meade said.

She lifted the map off the desk and held it with both hands. The map was torn in a corner that might have held some identifying information. The markings on the map itself indicated that it was a coastline, but there was no indication of what the map actually represented. Significant coastal emplacements—such as a large building or a lighthouse—and identified navigational information, such as rock formations and depth, were also items on the map. In the lower left-hand corner of the map were the initials "SW."

"Julia, did the admiral ever have visitors when he was working with these maps?" Lucinda asked.

"Yes," she said. "Occasionally, there were people who came and went."

"Do you remember any of them?"

"No, not really. Most of them were naval officers in uniform, and mostly what they did was bring him items or take with them things that he was sending to other people."

"But you do not remember any specifics about them?"

"Not really," she said, "but there was one person who stood out from the others. He was a civilian, not a Navy man."

"What do you remember about him?"

"He was a very distinguished-looking colored gentleman."

"Sylvester Watkins?" Meade asked.

"Yes, that's him."

Lucinda picked up the map and showed Julia the initials in the lower left-hand corner. "When we first saw this, we thought it might mean 'South West.' What do you think it means?"

Julia stared at the map for a few seconds. "I think it means Sylvester Watkins," she said. "I think he is somebody who would know something about this map—and something about what the admiral was doing."

Lucinda didn't speak, but she caught Meade's eye. Her brow raised just slightly. It wasn't skepticism—it was recognition. *This girl has a mind,* she was thinking. *Let's not underestimate her.*

Julia gathered her things. Her manner was polite, respectful, but she didn't wait to be dismissed. She moved with independence. Lucinda noticed it. Julia paused at the door as if recalling something critical.

"Mr. Meadows, I almost forgot," she said, a bit flustered at herself. "I saw you leave the house today and hail a carriage. Did you happen to notice anything across the street—across Massachusetts Avenue?"

Meade shook his head. "No, I didn't. What did I miss?"

"There was a man standing there—I'm pretty sure he had on a sailor's uniform—and he was watching you. Once you were in your carriage, he followed you down the street for as far as I could see."

"A man in a sailor's uniform?" Meade asked. "Was he an old guy or somebody pretty young?"

"An older gentleman, I think."

Meade turned to Lucinda and said, *"Burley O'Malley."*

Lucinda was no longer thinking just about the admiral. Her eyes lingered on the closed door after Julia left. *That one bears watching,* she thought.

17: Dinner at the Imperial

"I LOVED HIM," MARY Mae Radford said. She looked at her plate of food without interest. She had barely eaten anything since she and Hubert Meadows had sat down together. "You know how Ezra could be—demanding, difficult, and distant."

"He could also be determined," Hubert said, continuing with the alliteration.

"The demanding part I could manage," she said, "and the difficult part I could ignore. It was the distant part that always got to me."

"Ezra was a sailor, Mary Mae," Hubert said. "His heart was always out to sea, even in those times when he had shore duty."

Mary Mae sighed. "He hadn't had a command in more than a dozen years. He had become one of the Navy bureaucrats, and I don't think that ever sat well with him."

"No, I don't think it did either. Still, his knowledge and experience—his determination to do the best he could for the Navy—made him, at least in my mind, more valuable than anything else he had done in the years before."

"I appreciate your saying that, Hubert," Mary Mae said. "I really do."

They lapsed into a few moments of silence.

Mary Mae glanced again at the untouched food in front of her.

I should eat something, she thought, *but I can't summon the appetite—not tonight.*

Finally, she said, "So where do we go from here?"

Hubert's eyebrows furrowed, and the expression on his face turned grim. "Ezra's death has told us one thing for sure: whatever he was involved in was serious business—so serious that people were willing to murder to find out exactly what it was."

"And you have an idea about that, don't you?"

Hubert sat there, silent and expressionless.

"That's what I thought," Mary Mae said. "You and your friends."

"Me and my friends?"

"Don't play coy with me, Hubert, especially not now. I know a thing or two, and I'm pretty sure I know what you've been up to."

Again, Hubert was silent.

"We've been friends for too long, Hubert. We go back a very long way—more than some of these kids can know or understand. You're always behind the scenes, turning the screws, flipping the levers, pulling the strings. Don't sit there and try to tell me differently."

The dining room of the Imperial Hotel was nearly empty. Mary Mae and Hubert sat in a quiet corner, partially obscured by a giant column that held up the entire building. The air carried the aroma of roasted meat and sherry. Soft gaslight pooled across white tablecloths. A waiter moved like a shadow past the tall potted palms.

Hubert had requested that particular table to shield Mary Mae from any prying eyes or wagging tongues that might see her out with a non-family friend on the night of her husband's funeral. It was something that he did without saying anything or telling her about it, but she knew exactly why they were sitting where they were.

He still looks out for me, she thought, *even when I don't ask him to.*

She knew him so well. She knew that no matter how much persuasive cajoling she could manage that evening, he would not tell her everything he knew, so she changed tactics—or, as her mom might say, she shifted her sails.

"That son of yours is an impressive young man," she said. "He is well known around town. He's the best reporter in the city."

Hubert's expression shifted slightly. There was a glint of pride in the way he looked, but again, he did not give away much.

"And your daughter, Lucinda—I have met her a couple of times. She is more beautiful than any girl ought to be, and one of the most intelligent young women I have ever met."

The look of pride on Hubert's face was now unguarded.

"So how are these two young people going to help us?" she said.

"Those two kids," Hubert said, "they have their mother in their faces and in every fiber of their being. Sometimes I look at them and wonder where they came from."

"They have a good bit of you in them too, Hubert. That's probably the part you don't recognize."

They both took comfort in the relief of laughter. They shared a genuine friendship that was only slightly tinged with the regret of knowing that, at one point in their lives, it could have been much more.

"What makes you think Lucinda is going to be involved in this?"

Again, Mary Mae brushed aside his remark. "Need I keep reminding you, Hubert, that I know a thing or two about this town and who's in it? You're not the only one who has information, you know. I know how Meade and Lucinda work together. That's one of the things I probably know more about than you do."

Hubert sighed, an expression of defeat on this particular battlefield.

"I don't particularly want Lucinda mixed up in all this," he said. "But what I want doesn't seem to count for much with those two. Lucinda is smart as a flock of owls, but her major asset is that she is the one person that Meade will listen to. She can keep him going in the right direction. That seems to be beyond my talents these days."

Mary Mae wasn't finished. "But the question still stands: are you going to give Meade the help he needs to get to the bottom of all this?"

"Listen, Mary Mae," Hubert said with some animation, "I don't know who killed Ezra or why he was killed. If I had any idea about that, I would certainly say so."

"But you do know something."

"What I know is not going to help Meade—or Lucinda—at this point," he said. "Besides, Meade and I have a difficult relationship. We always have. He sees me as an interfering old coot."

"Is he wrong about that?"

"Not entirely," Hubert confessed. "The boy can be so mule-headed at times."

"I wonder which side of the family that comes from."

Hubert gave her a look that said he didn't need her sarcasm. He wasn't going to be completely cowed by anyone, even a strong-willed woman like Mary Mae Radford.

"Okay, Mary Mae," he said, "it's your turn. What is it that you know that you haven't said yet?"

Mary Mae looked at him steely-eyed. Hubert held the stare. She finally looked away. This wasn't her game.

"I suppose, Hubert, that I know plenty of things," she said. "I know that Ezra has been involved in a lot of fights over the past decade. He's always been so forward-looking. He's wanted the Navy to modernize in every way. He opposed training new officers in sailing techniques. A bunch of the old salts stood mightily against that. *'Violates our traditions,'* they kept saying."

She looked at her half-full glass of wine but resisted picking it up.

"And Ezra—well, he's a lot like you, Hubert—he wasn't much for diplomacy. He believed things and believed in things, and he didn't mind ruffling the feathers on some of these old birds."

Hubert smiled at the thought and the comparison.

"Ezra made a lot of enemies. I could name names, but I'm not sure that would do Meade any good. All I know, really, is what I told him this afternoon. The big change in Ezra occurred when he started working on something he wouldn't talk about. I just hope Meade can find out what that was."

Hubert picked at the dessert the waiter brought to the table.

"Meade's smart, determined, and resourceful," Hubert said. "He's already been looking into all of this. You and I may think we've been holding back information. My guess is Meade knows a lot more than he's letting on right now—maybe more than we know."

Hubert took a sip of the wine that had been served with their dinner.

"What I meant when I said Meade was resourceful and determined was that he knows how to think on his feet, assess his situation, and get himself out of danger if necessary."

Hubert poured himself another glass of wine from the bottle the waiter had left on the table. He offered some to Mary Mae, but she shook her head and covered her glass with her hand.

"Back in December 1864," Hubert said, "things were pretty wild in Nashville. Lincoln had won reelection, and most people believed the South was almost defeated, but there was still some fight left, and we all knew it. Confederates were working their way toward Nashville, and Union troops were all over the place."

"About that time, this colored kid showed up on our doorstep. His name was Josef, and he had run away from some family down in middle Tennessee and somehow made it up to Nashville. I'm not sure how old he was—maybe twelve. Meade was about ten at the time."

"Well, Josef had come to find his brother, who was a member of one of the colored troops serving under General Thomas. Secessionists were everywhere, and it really wasn't safe for this kid to be wandering around, so I decided that we should sneak him out of town on one of my lumber boats heading downstream on the Cumberland River toward the Ohio—that would put him in safe country."

"But the kid was determined to find his brother. He and Meade quickly struck up a friendship, and of course, Meade took his side and decided that he had a plan that was better than mine."

"That December was cold as the dickens, with an ice storm that blew through Nashville around that time. It didn't matter to Josef or Meade. Early one morning, they packed up their coats and boots, put some food in a bag, and Meade had promised Josef that he could find the unit where his brother was serving. So, without telling anybody, they took off."

"When I found out they had gone, I was furious. I sent out some men to try to find them, but they had no luck. Any day, we expected the Confederates to strike, and I knew Meade would get himself right in the middle of it."

"As it later panned out, Josef and Meade had rowed across the

Cumberland in a small boat and had taken off down Franklin Pike, asking anybody they could find where the 102nd Colored Division was located. By God, if they didn't find them."

"The trouble was, that unit was suited up and ready to march, and they really didn't have time to fool with two kids. So Josef persuaded his brother to give them both uniforms. Meade took a quick lesson in drum rolls and decided, for an afternoon at least, he would become a soldier."

"Well, you know how the army is—'hurry up and wait.' So, as soon as they got ready to go, they stood down. By that time, the commander of the unit had discovered the kids. Josef was kind of a big kid, so he decided that he could stay and be some sort of adjunct to the colonel. Meade, however, as you can imagine, just didn't fit in. When he realized they weren't going to let him stay, he told the colonel he could make it back home by himself."

"And you know, that's exactly what he did. It was long after dark before he got back home, and he had to talk his way through a number of situations and checkpoints, but he made it. I, of course, was still furious and raged until I was blue in the face. But Meade stood his ground. He told me I was wrong, and he was right, and that would be the end of it. Then he stomped up to the kitchen, made himself something to eat, and took himself to bed."

Mary Mae listened, fascinated. "That's quite a story," she said once Hubert had finished.

Hubert picked up the wine bottle and poured more into his glass, then made another offer to Mary Mae; this time, she accepted it.

"Ever since that day," Hubert said, "Meade has been telling me that I am wrong." He settled back into his chair and gave out a mirthless laugh.

The two shared a few moments of silence, then engaged in some whispered small talk. The subjects were safe and comfortable. As they concentrated on each other, they did not realize that a third person was in their presence. A small movement alerted them to the fact.

Standing before them was a rather short, stocky man who was close to their age. Both Hubert and Mary Mae recognized him immediately.

"One of your friends, Hubert?" Mary Mae asked as she looked up.

Hubert stood up and shook the man's hand vigorously. *Of all the nights,* he thought. *What on earth brings him here now?*

"As I live and breathe, Commander Tower," he said. "It's very good to see you, very good indeed."

18: The Diplomat

THE APRIL EVENING HAD turned from sunny and warm to cold, damp, and dark. The diplomat felt the dampness keenly as he made his way along the banks of Rock Creek through Oak Hill Cemetery. The small lantern he carried offered light for only a few steps; he had already tripped once and had learned from that to take smaller steps and be more cautious. His progress through the cemetery was slow and painful.

Why did the American insist on meeting here? the diplomat grumbled. At least in a dingy bar, as unpleasant as that was, he could sit and drink the almost undrinkable beer they served. The bar would've offered some warmth.

There was no warmth here. The note from the American demanding the meeting had shown up on his desk late that afternoon, of course disrupting the plans he had made for the evening—plans that included a reception at the Belgian Embassy, where the beautiful young wife of a Belgian attaché would be waiting for him. She knew all the rooms in the embassy where they could meet in private. She kept the keys to those rooms just under the deeply scooped décolletage of her dress. When they managed to maneuver themselves to be alone, she invited him to reach down into that dress. Whatever key he found was the room they would retire to; it was a little game they played.

He wondered if they would be playing it tonight. Late that afternoon, a typewritten note had appeared on his desk demanding his presence at this time and at this godforsaken place. His first reaction was to ignore the note. But this operation was too important. It meant too much to his superiors—and to him personally.

He comforted himself with the thought that if this meeting were a short one, he would still have time to get back to the embassy. As his mind wandered to that possibility, he again tripped over one of the small tombstones. This time, he was able to catch himself before he hit the ground. He dropped his lantern and was reaching around on the ground for it when he heard the voice.

"Having trouble?"

The American appeared before him. He had not heard the footsteps of anyone approaching.

The diplomat found his lantern, picked it up, and held it high. The American was far enough away that only the figure of a person appeared. A dark hood covered the head. No facial features were discernible. The only thing the diplomat could tell about the American was that the figure was shorter than he would have expected. The voice was deep and commanding.

"What do you want?" the diplomat said, not trying to disguise his irritability.

There was silence from the American, and the diplomat took a step closer.

"Stay where you are," the voice said. The diplomat looked up and saw that the American had moved back several steps.

"I want the money you failed to give me the last time we met," the American said.

"I gave you what we had agreed upon."

"Yes, but you didn't give me what you had—what you were will-ing to give me. I need that money."

The American was clever, the diplomat conceded. His govern-ment had indeed given him permission to pay whatever the cost was, as long as the American succeeded. Still, it was worth a bit of an argument.

"What do you need the money for?"

"I have expenses. I have to pay people. This thing is not easy, you know."

The voice of the American had become low and soft, almost in-discernible, but there was a determination behind it that the diplo-mat could not escape.

"What is your plan? How is that proceeding?"

"We'll talk about plans and proceedings after you leave the money on top of the tombstone, right beside where you're standing," the American said.

The diplomat thought about what awaited him at the Belgian Embassy that evening and decided that the time for argument was finished. He slipped his hand inside one of his vest pockets and pulled out an envelope. He held it up to the light so the American could see it, then placed it on top of the tombstone as designated.

"This is your last demand for money until we see some results," he said with some bravado.

The American made a noise—he could not tell if it was contempt or concession.

"Now tell me," the diplomat said, "how much closer are you to getting those maps that we want?"

"Plans are in place," the American said, "and things are about to happen."

"Is that all you can tell me?"

"That's all for right now. You will know what you need to know when you need to know it."

"That's not satisfactory," the diplomat said with as much authority as he could muster. "The people in my government, the ones who are giving you this money, need to know that you are making progress. Do you know where the maps are?"

"The people in your government know the maps exist," the American said. "They also know that it's too dangerous for them to try to find them. They know they need somebody like me. If you have somebody else in mind to do the job, I will be on my way."

The American and the diplomat stood perfectly still. They could both hear the rushing water of Rock Creek just below where they were standing.

"That's what I thought," the American said quietly. "I do not know where the maps are. What I am doing is setting up a way that I can find out."

"And how are you doing that?"

"First, by causing some confusion," the American said. "Confusion creates opportunities. There may be an opportunity opening up."

"What opportunity is that?"

"I'm not going to tell you that. There are too many chattering mouths in your embassy, and your constant liaisons don't inspire a lot of confidence."

This American is unlike any other agent I have ever worked with, the diplomat thought, shocked by the American's boldness in spying on him. He had never had an agent turn the tables like that. He was impressed.

"Is that what all this money I am giving you is for—spying on me?"

There was a bit of amusement in the American's voice. "Maybe," the American responded, the tone light yet enigmatic.

The diplomat could not resist the opportunity this information offered him.

"How was the admiral's funeral?"

This time the American was silent.

"So you've been spying on me as well?"

"Maybe," the diplomat said, in the same voice the American had just used.

In the ensuing silence, the diplomat sensed some slight movement on the American's part.

"Okay, let's quit playing games. Call your dogs off. They're just going to get in the way. If I find they're still hanging around, the whole thing is off, and your government is going to blame you for wasting their money."

The diplomat did not respond.

The American continued, "I can tell you this much: most people have accepted the fact that the admiral committed suicide, but there are a few people, inside and outside the Navy, who don't believe that."

"And that's your opportunity?"

"It could very well be."

The diplomat bent down to pick up his lantern where he had placed it before putting the money on the tombstone.

"Are we finished here?" he asked.

"There's one more thing," the American said. "We need a plan in place to get me out of the country."

"In case things go wrong?"

"Whether they go right or wrong, it is not likely that I'm going to be successful without my identity being discovered by somebody. And if that happens, I need to disappear."

"Disappear to where?"

"Someplace warm and friendly, where I can take advantage of your country's generosity."

The diplomat thought that over for a moment, then said in a smooth and comforting voice, "I think that can be arranged."

"Good," the American said. "Now, I think it's time that you should run along to your embassy party. Mustn't keep the lady waiting. I'm sure you two have your secrets to share. Just be sure our secret stays as dark as this graveyard. Sharing that secret would be very unhealthy. Lethal, in fact."

Stunned, the diplomat nearly lost his balance. This meeting was supposed to be one where he was in control. But now, he was being dismissed—and dismissed with a threat.

The diplomat turned and stumbled through the darkness, finally reaching his carriage. The driver and horse had been patiently awaiting his return. He muttered something about going to the Belgian Embassy. They seemed to understand and moved accordingly.

Once inside, the diplomat kept hearing the last words the American had spoken. The words were a threat. Of that, there was no doubt. But the sound... something about that voice seemed odd and out of place, like it had come from a different human being.

Lethal. That word stuck in his brain. One person had already died. What the American had said clearly indicated there would be more.

19: Athletic Park

NATHAN TOWER THOUGHT OF himself as a simple man. His years at sea had taught him that a chessboard, a few books, and an open sky were all he really needed in life. Pursuing enemy warships and giving battle provided the excitement and memories he needed to sustain himself.

But wars don't last forever—at least not the shooting wars. When the Civil War ended and ship after ship in the Navy was decommissioned, life at sea no longer seemed a viable option. However, Nathan was adaptable; he could change with the times, he told himself. *Just give me an opportunity—that's all I need.*

That opportunity came when he joined the diplomatic service as a military attaché. His first posting was the American Embassy in London, a premier assignment. It was an easy trip to places like Portsmouth, where the British, unlike their American cousins, were building up their Navy, not taking it apart. He watched with fascination as the ships of the British Navy took shape and eventually sailed out to sea.

From London, he went to Paris, where he found the culture and customs of France to be totally different from anything he had ever experienced. It was not a difference that made him comfortable, yet there was something to be learned from the French; they were not always what they seemed. In Paris, Nathan began to understand the concepts of espionage and counterespionage. He acquired an acute appreciation of intelligence and how valuable it was in a world of competing national interests.

In Paris, he also acquired a wife—her name was Francine. He congratulated himself when he thought of her, remembering her name. She was from a wealthy, titled family, and her marriage to a rather low-ranking American naval officer was considered by many of her acquaintances as exotic. Nathan did not think of himself as exotic and soon tired of playing that role. Even more quickly, Francine tired of playing the wife of an American and reintegrated herself into the Parisian life for which she had been born. They parted amicably, even before he left Paris.

He occasionally thought of Francine and wondered where she was, what she was doing, and—without jealousy—who she was with. None of that seemed to make much difference to him now that he was back in Washington. After France, he spent a couple of years in Vienna and then three years in Berlin. Those years demonstrated to him, in ways he could never have imagined, the interesting and intriguing aspects of espionage. It is fair to say that he became a student of this ancient discipline, but he was more than a student—he was an advocate.

When he finally returned to Washington, he was still the simple man in personal habits that he had always been. He was convinced that the United States would play a significant role in world affairs during the next decades. To play that role, the government had to acquire the skills and techniques of espionage and counterespionage that he had observed in Europe, and that had become an art form among the great European powers.

So Nathan Tower joined the Office of Naval Intelligence in the low-level position of Director of Naval Attachés. His only official duty was to train and assign the naval attachés who were posted to American embassies around the world. Other officers of his rank and experience would have chafed at such a seemingly inconsequential position.

But Nathan had a different attitude. The assignment was the perfect cover for building and operating an intelligence and espionage network. This network would protect the nation from the intrigues of foreign powers. It would gather military, industrial, and governmental intelligence and use it to the advantage of the United States.

All of these thoughts, and many more, flowed through Nathan Tower's mind as he sat by himself in the stands of the Seventh Street Athletic Park in Northwest Washington, awaiting the start of that day's game for the Washington Nationals baseball team. The April afternoon was sunny and slightly cool, the March wind not having stopped blowing completely.

Nathan had arrived at the stadium early enough to watch batting practice. He enjoyed observing the individual hitters and how they approached their task. Although they were all trying to hit the thrown ball from a pitcher standing 60 or so feet away, each approached the task differently. Some leaned out, some leaned in, some stood straight. Some held the bat at the very end seeking the most powerful swing, while others moved their hands up the bat to gain control over where the ball would go when hit.

Nathan Tower was a simple man in the middle years of his life. He had grown to love two things deeply: espionage and baseball.

Most of the hours of every day of his life were spent attempting to figure out what the enemies of the United States were doing to gain an advantage for their own nation. When he thought he had that figured out, he then attempted to come up with ways to stop them and to counter their moves.

Espionage is like chess. The games can be won or lost, but there's always another game.

Baseball provided Nathan with both relief from his main activity and instruction about it. As he watched the batters line up and take their hits, there was always a different approach, always a different attitude, and often a different goal.

Tower was dressed as an ordinary workman, in a loose-fitting light shirt and denim slacks. He wore a soft felt hat. Seated along the first baseline, next to one of the pillars supporting the stadium's roof, he was positioned to observe the game and the field while also being able to obscure himself quickly if necessary. He had arrived early enough that the crowd was initially sparse, but the stadium had since begun to fill up.

He was watching the infield take their practice turns when he sensed the presence of someone approaching. A man in a suit sat down beside him—not someone dressed to enjoy a baseball game.

"Hubert," he said, keeping his eye on the infield.

"Nathan," his new companion responded.

They sat together in silence for the next five minutes, as the seats around them began to fill. The stadium was not crowded. The attendance would be light this afternoon, and Hubert Meadows and Nathan Tower looked merely like two gentlemen seated next to each other, ready to enjoy the game.

Finally, Tower spoke. "I see you dressed appropriately for the occasion."

Hubert harrumphed. "I see no point in this silly game."

"Hubert," Tower said in mock surprise, "this is baseball, my friend—the American game. How can you sit there and say that?"

They still had not looked at one another directly.

Hubert harrumphed again.

Tower loved to needle Hubert about his lack of interest in baseball. In fact, Hubert was one of the few men Tower knew who had not developed an avid affection for the game—Hubert's three-piece suit spoke loudly of that deficiency.

During the baseball season, Tower often insisted that Hubert meet him at the game, not just to annoy Hubert, but also because Tower was unlikely to be noticed in the crowd.

"Your pitcher seems to be throwing strikes today," Hubert said.

It had not taken long for Hubert and Tower to develop some coded messages, just in case there were any eavesdroppers around. Hubert had just informed Tower that the secret bank account, which Tower used to fund many of his operations, had been replenished.

"Well," Tower said, nodding at the pitcher, "we'll see what he's got for our game today."

"Which team are we playing today?"

"The team from St. Louis," Tower said, indicating to Hubert that Spain was the current adversary.

Hubert did not like this cryptic code-talking. It made him self-conscious. He thought of himself as a direct, plain-spoken man, and this didn't feel right.

Hubert leaned back in his seat while Tower maintained his concentration on the field, his elbows resting on his thighs as he looked carefully around the stadium.

"The home team is about to take the field," he said.

Hubert wasn't sure if that was a code or just a description of what was about to happen. Suddenly, right in front of them, players uniformed with 'W' on their caps and shirts emerged from the dugout and started running onto the field. Immediately, the crowd rose with a cheer, and from then on, the noise level increased. Hubert was relieved; this meant that he and Tower could finally talk to each other in plain English, not in the code that Tower seemed to love.

"Are all of our mutual friends on board?" Tower asked.

Hubert knew he was referring to what they privately called The Committee. These were the people who were funding much of Tower's operation. These were the people who recognized—often with Tower's persuasion—that the United States was woefully behind in the great game of chess that was being played by the world's major powers.

"Everyone is accounted for," Hubert said. "Eventually, they're going to want an accounting from you."

Tower nodded. "As always," he said, "I'll tell you what I can."

A noise rose from the crowd as the first batter from the St. Louis team stroked a single to left field on the third pitch.

"That's not a good sign," Tower murmured, knowing he was probably talking to himself since Hubert wasn't paying attention to the game.

As the next batter approached the plate, Hubert spoke up, "You know that Mary Mae has asked Meade to look into the admiral's death."

Tower glanced at Hubert. "Yes, I know that. I also know that he had an interest in all of that before she asked."

"How do you know that?"

"I have lots of different sources of information. Besides, Meade hasn't made it any secret, particularly around the Navy. He's been asking a lot of questions."

The next batter took two balls, both high and wide. The crowd groaned; this pitcher was supposed to be the Senators' ace, and he wasn't looking so good today.

"Has Meade told you anything about what he found?" Tower asked.

"Meade doesn't talk to me very much."

"What has he told Lucinda?"

"How do you know he talks to Lucinda?" Hubert looked mildly surprised.

"I know lots of things."

The Nationals' pitcher threw a strike, and a sarcastic cheer went up from the crowd.

"Lucinda hasn't told me very much either," Hubert admitted. "Just bits and pieces. I've been picking up some rumors about the admiral. The thing that concerns me is that I have a feeling Meade's walking into a danger zone."

The next pitch was a wild ball that got past the catcher and went to the backstop. The runner on first took second without even a slide, drawing groans from the crowd.

Tower turned and looked directly at Hubert. "He is getting into a danger zone," he said. "It's serious business. Whoever is behind all of this has already proven they'll do their worst. The fact that the admiral is dead tells us that."

"I was afraid of that," Hubert said. "Is it time for me to tell Meade to come see you?"

Tower shook his head. "Meade is a smart, tough guy. We've got eyes on him. I'll try to do what we can to make sure he doesn't get hurt. But I can't guarantee anything."

"I understand that."

The next pitch resulted in a loud crack of the bat. The ball sailed over second base into the gap between the center and left fielder. The runner on second scored easily, and the batter, one of St. Louis's speedsters, made it into third base well ahead of a weak throw from the outfield.

"Well, it's only the top of the first," Tower said with some resignation. "We still have a whole ballgame to go."

Tower looked to his left and found that he was talking to an empty space. Hubert had left without notice or ceremony.

On the field, the Nationals' manager had called time and was slowly trudging out to the pitcher's mound to talk with the pitcher and catcher. This was one of the things Tower loved about baseball. The gaps in the action gave him a chance to think, and this time, as happened frequently, his imagination took over.

Tower leaned forward in his seat, resting his elbows on his knees and lacing his fingers together. His eyes narrowed slightly as he fixed them on third base, his mind slipping into an imagined scenario.

He sees himself as the team's manager on his way to the mound. He notes something about the way the St. Louis runner slides into third base, pops straight up, and looks toward home plate. He also detects an arrogance in the glint of his eye, an arrogance that seems to say, "I can steal home plate if I can get a jump on that pitcher."

Tower, the manager, wants to take advantage of that arrogance.

Tower walks out to the mound and calls all the infielders in. He tells the pitcher, "Whatever you do, don't look at that guy on third base. Instead, I want your next two pitches to be balls. Don't give the batter anything he can touch. Take your time. Fool around between each pitch. But whatever you do, don't look at the guy on third base. We want to make him think you're not paying attention to him."

He turns to the third baseman. "After he throws the second ball, I want you to take a couple of steps toward the bag. After the pitcher gets the ball back, he's going to fool around the mound for a few seconds. Then, he's going to turn to you and fire the ball. Be ready to catch it and put the tag on the runner, who will be too far off base to get back in time."

He turns back to the pitcher and says, "Got it?" "Got it, coach."

He turns to the third baseman and says, "Got it?" "Got it, coach."

Thirty seconds later, the runner is picked off by a snap throw from the pitcher. The rally of the visiting team is over.

Tower blinked and shifted slightly in his seat, the real game reasserting itself around him.

Back on the field, the pitcher threw his next pitch right over the plate, and the batter connected for a solid single that drove in another run for the St. Louis team.

The crowd groaned, and Tower sank back into his seat and sighed dejectedly.

20: Benny MacBain

IT TOOK MEADE MEADOWS only about four days to track down Benny MacBain. He found Benny in a rough-and-tumble bar on the south side of Annapolis. It was only a few blocks from the grounds of the Naval Academy, but a world away from the military order and spit-and-polish that was standard for that institution.

The April evening's darkness had set in, and the bar, misnamed *The Captain's Cabin*, had not invested heavily in indoor lighting. Meade could see well enough to know that one corner of the bar was occupied by sailors and stevedores involved in a serious and loud game of poker. In another corner was a dartboard into which darts were being flung with no great accuracy. There, too, was noise, multiple glasses of beer, and gambling.

The Captain's Cabin was woefully short of captains.

Benny sat by himself in a dark third corner, nursing a solitary glass of beer and looking like he wasn't nearly finished with his alcohol consumption that evening. Benny looked steadily at Meade but gave no sign of recognition.

Meade stopped at the bar and ordered two glasses of the establishment's best beer. He picked up the glasses and walked over to Benny's table. He set them down and then put himself in the chair opposite Benny.

"Are you my long-lost nephew?" Benny said.

Meade had come down by train that afternoon and had spent the afternoon and early evening scouring the waterfront bars asking for Benny. When the people he talked to bothered to inquire as to why he wanted to see Benny—whom they obviously knew—his cover story had been that he was Benny's long-lost nephew, giving them a line or two about an inheritance; most of the time, that was good enough.

"I'm the one. You must be my uncle," Meade said, a smile on his lips.

Benny was old and wizened. Meade estimated that he was in his seventies, at least; that's what he looked like, but Meade knew that years at sea can age you quickly. Benny was hunched over, a short, stocky guy, but his face and his eyes told any observant person that his mind was as sharp as a razor.

Benny got the joke. "So, what's this about my inheritance?" he asked Meade.

Meade smiled again. "Well, I'm sorry to tell you that your other nephews have spent it all."

Benny laughed heartily. "Now, what is it that I can do for you, Mr. Meadows?"

Meade showed surprise that Benny knew his name.

"This new navy that they've got going these days—it's still a pretty small world," Benny said. "The big topic of conversation is the old admiral's death, and it's no secret that you've been asking about it."

Meade raised his glass to the old admiral. Benny did the same.

With the glasses back on the table, Meade looked at Benny. "I'm trying to find out what got the admiral killed," he said.

Benny looked serious. "I don't know anything about that, Mr.

Meadows. I wish I did. Radford was a good man, and we go way back."

"You may know more than you realize," Meade said. "What can you tell me about Sylvester Watkins?"

Now it was Benny's turn to look surprised. "Stoney? Stoney Watkins?" A broad smile covered Benny's face. "Stoney Watkins was the best there ever was. If I had to pick a crew to put out to sea with, Stoney would be the first one."

This was the reason Meade had come to Annapolis to talk to Benny MacBain. When Lucinda, Julia, and he had decided that the initials on the map were those of Sylvester Watkins, his first instinct was to find Watkins immediately and talk to him. However, this instinct was quickly overcome by his reporter's experience. He needed to find out something about Watkins so that when he did talk to him, he would be prepared to ask good questions—and possibly know what kind of answers Watkins was giving him.

So, he had spent several days in Washington talking to people about the admiral's death, but also bringing up the name Sylvester Watkins more than once. Those who spoke to him had said that when he was in the Navy, Watkins and Benny MacBain worked together and seemed to be good friends.

Benny MacBain had served on the *USS Kearsarge* along with First Lieutenant Ezra Radford and then-Seaman Sylvester Watkins. He was part of the gunnery team commanded by Radford that had an important role in sinking the legendary *CSS Alabama*. Meade had looked up his record in the Navy Department and found that for his work in that day's battle, he and 18 others had received the Congressional Medal of Honor.

The name that was not on that list was Sylvester Watkins, and

Meade had an idea about why that was the case.

"Have you talked to Stoney lately?" Benny asked. "How is he? It's been a while since I've been able to get up to Washington to see him."

Meade told Benny about Watkins delivering one of the eulogies at the admiral's funeral. "He looks good and sounded good," Meade said. "He seems to be prospering."

"That's great," Benny said. "Stoney was one sharp dude—a lot sharper than I was."

Sylvester and Benny's paths took wildly different directions after the war. Once the war was over, the Navy began reducing its ships, armament, and personnel immediately. Sylvester was one of the first to be sent packing. Benny was able to hang on for a few more years, but those who knew him said that he had finally been discharged due to excessive drunkenness—one source that Meade spoke with said the drinking was just an excuse to get rid of him. In the early 1870s, the Navy was still downsizing, and Benny was a victim of that more than anything else.

"If ever there was a man meant for the sea, it was Stoney," Benny said.

"What do you mean by that?"

"Stoney could read a navigational map and tell you exactly where we were, particularly if the coastline was in view."

"There was nothing unusual about that, was there?"

"No, not about that. But a lot of our maps were old and out of date. He could tell you what was wrong with them."

"How did he do that?"

"Beats me," Benny said. "None of us could really figure that out. Stoney seemed to have a sense of these things. He could tell you without looking at a chart, and if the chart was wrong and he said it was, we learned to trust him more than the maps that we had."

"What else do you remember about him?"

"He didn't seem to be afraid of anything. He would climb up a mast, all the way up to the top just to get a better view of things. And when he came down, if he was looking at the coastline, he could draw it out pretty near the way it was."

"He had that kind of memory for coastlines?"

"Not just coastlines. Once he was up on a mast and could see, he could tell you everything that was there."

That's quite a talent he had.

Benny took a long swallow of his beer. "Something else about Stoney you need to know—he got a lot of bad treatment, particularly from the officers, because of the fact that he was colored. The guy who stood up for him the most was Ezra Radford. Being enlisted, I weren't supposed to notice that kind of stuff, but Radford made some powerful enemies when he faced down officers who were trying to abuse Stoney. He really put himself on the line lots of times."

Meade's jaw tightened. *They always said Radford was uncompromising—but no one ever said it was because he had the guts to stand up for someone like Watkins. That explains a lot. And it means there's even more at stake here than I thought.*

"Tell me about the battle between the *Kearsarge* and the *Alabama*," Meade said.

Benny launched into a long, detailed description. "The *Kearsarge* spent a month tracking down the *Alabama*. We were a better ship with a better crew and better guns," he said. "The *Alabama* kept slipping through our fingers. Finally, we had her cornered off the coast of France. She was trapped and she knew it."

Benny seemed to relish this part of the story. "She finally poked her head out from that port, and I will say she put up the best fight she could, but we had her outgunned, and it didn't take long to put her under. The most fun was pulling those Confederates out from the drink and letting them see what a real ship was like."

"You got yourself a medal for what you did that day," Meade said.

Benny acted like he didn't think that was important. "Yeah, a bunch of us got medals. None of us cared about that much."

"But one of you didn't get a medal," Meade said.

Benny raised his eyebrow. "You're talking about Stoney. Yeah, he should've gotten a medal, and he didn't. Some of us weren't real happy about that. He didn't seem to care much, but it was Radford who raised hell. He had written a commendation, but it got stopped as it went up the line. He raised hell, and I suspect that didn't make him any friends."

"In other words, he made enemies by going to bat for Sylvester Watkins," Meade said.

"Big-time enemies," Benny said. "Enemies that never forgot and never forgave."

21: Sylvester Watkins

Early in the morning after his talk with Benny McBain, Meade viewed downtown Washington out the windows of the Beltline streetcar as it made its way north to within a few blocks of Howard University.

Meade enjoyed streetcars. He liked seeing the people getting on and off, pondering where they might be going and what their day might be like. Occasionally, he would meet someone friendly enough to strike up a conversation, and more than once, those conversations had provided him with good feature story material for his newspaper, *The Washington Beacon*.

On this particular morning, he was on the streetcar somewhat earlier than usual, and it was populated by the working-class people of Washington, D.C. These were not the politicians or the big-money bankers and financiers that his newspaper paid so much attention to. These were the people who kept the city running. Many of them had been born and raised in Washington. Some were immigrants from other countries, seeking their fortune in the nation's capital and beyond. Many had come from the South, where the war two decades before had destroyed lives and livelihoods. Many who got on and off the streetcar that morning were of different races—white, Black, Asian, Latin American—and Meade was impressed by how they all seemed to be working together to make the city function.

Meade had returned very late the previous evening from Annapolis. When he entered his house on Connecticut Avenue and walked into the study, he found a note from Lucinda: *Talk to me in the morning as soon as possible,* the note said.

Under normal circumstances, Meade would have waited until Lucinda was up and had a long discussion with her about his interview with Benny McBain and about whatever it was that she wanted to discuss. Instead, on this particular morning, Meade left early before anybody had gotten up. Two things drove him to make this unusual move:

One was that he was anxious to find and talk to Sylvester Watkins. After his discussion with Benny McBain, Meade was convinced that Watkins could indeed provide important information about the death of the admiral and about whatever it was the admiral had been working on at the time of his death.

The second reason for his early departure—one he considered not nearly as noble—was that he wanted to avoid any conversation with his father. As he usually did when he visited Washington, Hubert stayed in the house on Connecticut Avenue. There was certainly plenty of room for him, and even if Meade had objected—and he never had—Lucinda would have vetoed any objection and insisted that there was always a place in their house for their father. She was indeed right, and Meade knew it.

Still, conversation with the old man is like sailing into a headwind. You have to tack around every opinion he throws at you before you can chart your own course. Meade felt like it was especially so now that he had been asked by Mary Mae Radford to look into the admiral's death. Hubert would no doubt want to know what Meade was finding out and would ask a dozen questions before their first cup of coffee. Along with the questions would come, inevitably, the advice and direction that Hubert always insisted on giving his son. The crux of the matter was that Meade wanted to go his own way, make his own mistakes, and gain his own successes. Hubert, for all of his good qualities, his generosity, and his courage, never seemed to quite understand or accept that about Meade.

It occurred to Meade, only briefly, that even on the Beltline he could not get away from Hubert completely. Hubert was one of the line's chief investors and on its board of directors. Hubert was making a ton of money off his investment. Hubert was one of those people who never made a wrong move financially.

The Beltline reached its northernmost point on Ninth Street, then turned east for two blocks, and then north on Seventh Street. Meade watched as the campus of Howard University came into view. In another two minutes, he was out on the street and walking onto the campus.

The Howard campus stretched over 73 acres, consisting of a large open field and one grand building the university called Main Hall. Several other wooden buildings surrounded it like little chicks gathering around a mother hen.

What was most impressive about the campus, however, was the number of people and the activities they produced by their coming and going this early in the day. Most of them, of course, were African American, but Meade, a white man who definitely stood out from the crowd, was not the only white person there.

Another thing a visitor might have noticed was that there were as many women as there were men—maybe more. When Howard opened its doors in 1867, anyone—male or female—was welcome.

It did not take long for Meade to discover where Sylvester Watkins was located. Mentioning his name brought glimmers of recognition that should not have surprised Meade—at least that's what he told himself as he made his way to the third floor of Main Hall and then down the hallway to the last door on the left, as he had been instructed. There was a nameplate on the door that read **Sylvester Watkins, Research Fellow**.

The door was open, so Meade stuck his head in and saw a very small outer office that led to something larger beyond. A pretty young female student sat at a desk that had been wedged in the corner of the outer office. She had dark skin, dark eyes, and plenty of dark hair that surrounded a delicate face with a turned-up nose and broad lips.

Meade might have mistaken her for a secretary, but her desk was not filled with secretarial materials. Instead, there were maps and charts that obscured the surface, and more maps and charts pinned up around the walls next to the desk. She was studying one of the charts on her desk intensely, so taken by it that she seemed a bit startled when Meade said, "Good morning."

She looked up at him with a wide smile that showed bright teeth and answered, "Good morning. How can I help you?"

"I'm looking for Sylvester Watkins. Is this his office?"

"Yes, it is," she said. "His office is right in there." She nodded toward the inner door. "You can go in there if you like. He's in right now."

Meade was taken with the girl's forwardness. It was as if she controlled the space they were in and was not about to concede anything to a white man who happened to intrude upon it.

He said, "Thank you," and walked into Watkins' office. Watkins had obviously heard the exchange in the outer office and was looking up toward the door when Meade walked in.

Meade started to introduce himself, but Watkins interrupted him. "I know who you are, Mr. Meadows. You are quite famous."

"Is that a compliment or an insult?" Meade said with a grin, showing he was trying to begin the conversation on a light note.

"It is neither, Mr. Meadows," Watkins said. "It is simply an observation."

Watkins had a low, sonorous voice with diction that told the listener he was careful and precise with the English language. Meade remembered that Watkins had spent his formative years at sea and wondered briefly why he did not sound more like a sailor, but dismissed the thought—it wasn't the question he had come to ask.

"What can I do for you, Mr. Meadows?"

Having been through a dozen scenarios of how this conversation might go, Meade still wasn't prepared. On the spur of the moment, he decided that rather than ask a question, he would make a statement.

"I talked to a friend of yours last night," Meade said, hoping for an effect.

Watkins, who had expected a question, seemed a bit taken aback. That was the effect Meade had hoped for.

"Benny McBain," Meade added.

Watkins' recognition of McBain's name was immediate; his face lit up. "My old pal Benny McBain. We called him Longneck."

"Longneck?"

Watkins laughed. "For obvious reasons. He had no neck whatsoever." And Watkins let out another laugh.

Watkins asked a series of questions about Benny: how he was, where he was, and how Meade had found him. Meade answered each one thoroughly and relayed comments that Benny had made about Watkins. "He said you were the best sailor he ever served with."

Watkins acknowledged the compliment.

"He also told me that you should have received the Congressional Medal of Honor at the same time he and the others in your gunnery crew did. But you were denied it because you are a Negro," Meade continued. "He said Ezra Radford went to bat for you, even made some enemies. But he also said you were willing to let it go."

Watkins sighed. "Mr. Meadows, you learn something while you are at war on the ocean. You learn to pick your battles and not to get into a fight you can't win."

He paused, then added, "That's something these kids around here have yet to learn. They want to fight every battle, win every victory. They haven't learned that life doesn't work that way."

Then he raised an eyebrow. "But you didn't come here to talk about Benny McBain."

"No, I didn't. But let me tell you something else that Benny said."

"What's that?"

"He said that he didn't think Ezra Radford killed himself."

Meade let that statement settle for a moment. Watkins looked at him steadily. Then he asked, "What do you think, Mr. Meadows?"

"I don't think the admiral killed himself either. What do you think?"

Watkins held his gaze. Meade had laid his cards on the table.

"I'm not surprised you think that. I understand you've been making inquiries."

So he's talking to people inside the Navy. Or someone close to it. That was something.

Watkins had just confirmed an important fact for Meade. He had just admitted that he was in active communication with people in the Navy—people other than Ezra Radford. That was something.

"Benny McBain told me you could read a navigational chart and a shoreline like no one he's ever sailed with," Meade said.

Watkins seemed to ignore the compliment. "And how did you come to be talking with Benny about that particular topic?"

"Because I asked him about it," Meade replied. "Because I heard your eulogy at the admiral's funeral. Because I've heard other people say the same thing."

Watkins nodded but wasn't going to elaborate further.

Watkins was proving to be cagier than Meade had hoped. It was time for a more direct approach.

"I've heard that you have been working on a secret navigational project for the Navy."

"I saw you at the funeral," he said, "and I saw your father. I have known him for years, you know."

Meade was determined not to get distracted, especially with talk of his father. It was time to throw a knockout punch.

"I understand you have been drawing new navigational charts," Meade said, his gaze fixed on Watkins' face, "and I know that the project involves not our coast, but that of a European country."

Meade kept his eyes on Watkins. "I understand the project involves new navigational charts. And not for our coast. For a European one."

It was a bluff. But Watkins froze.

Got him.

Meade had struck home, so he decided to soften the blow. "Look, Mr. Watkins. I'm really not trying to uncover any secrets. I don't believe the admiral killed himself. I think somebody murdered him. I'm just trying to find out why."

The muscles in Watkins' weather-beaten face visibly relaxed.

"You're right, Mr. Meadows. I, too, do not believe the admiral killed himself. Suicide is a stain on his memory that Ezra Radford does not deserve. I have been working on a project that is much as you described. It is a secret project, and I can't say much about it."

He paused for a moment and then continued. "Here's something that you are likely to find out if you just ask around campus, so I will save you some time. I was recently able to send a team of four of my geography students to Spain for three weeks. It was officially designated by the university as a field trip, and the money to pay for the trip came from a source that I cannot disclose."

Meade realized that this was the end of the interview. Watkins was not going to tell him anything else. He and Watkins spent another ten minutes in polite conversation about non-essential topics. Watkins asked about Hubert and was informed that Hubert was in good health.

"Please greet him for me, and tell him how much I would enjoy seeing him."

Meade promised to do so.

Meade thanked Watkins for his time and for the information and excused himself. When he walked through the small outer office, he was surprised to find it empty. He was also surprised to see a sealed note pinned to the doorframe at eye level so that he could not miss it. On the outside were the words, **MISTER MEADOWS**.

Meade took the note and found his way out of Main Hall.

When he reached the first large shade tree, he pulled the note out of his pocket, broke the seal, and opened it up. On the inside was this message:

"Take the Belt Line back south into Washington. After it turns onto Seventh Street, get off at the corner of T Street. I'll be waiting."

— ✦ —

22: Margaret Douglass

M EADE SAW HER FROM more than half a block away. The streetcar he was riding had only a few passengers. It was mid-morning, past the time when most people were already at work.

He rang the bell, and as the car slowed, he stepped off a few yards from the corner of T Street. The woman he had seen earlier that morning in Professor Sylvester Watkins' outer office stood waiting on the corner.

She walked up and offered her hand, which Meade took and shook gently. "My name is Margaret Douglass," she said.

"I'm very pleased to meet you. Again," Meade replied.

He glanced around to confirm what he already knew: this part of Washington, D.C., was populated mostly—but not entirely—by African Americans. There were a few white faces here and there, his being the most conspicuous, but nobody seemed to be paying him any mind.

No one except this pretty, delicate-looking young woman.

"I need to ask you something," he said. She looked at him expectantly. "How did you know I would be taking the streetcar? You saw me when I arrived at the campus this morning."

She laughed softly. "No, Mr. Meadows, that wasn't it," she said. "Actually, I was just guessing. Most white people who come to

Howard—those who aren't regulars—take the Beltline up from the city. That's because white carriage drivers often refuse to come this far uptown. And if you're white and driving your own carriage, you're afraid someone might steal your horse. So the sensible thing to do is take the streetcar."

Well, that makes uncomfortable sense, Meade thought.

Meade might have felt chastised, but she said it so matter-of-factly, even with amusement, that it came across not as criticism but simple observation—something every Black Washingtonian understood and few white residents ever thought about.

"If you don't mind," she continued, "I'd like you to walk with me a couple of blocks down T Street. There's something I want to talk to you about."

"Certainly," Meade said.

T Street was much like others surrounding the core of the city. It was lined with shops and businesses, some tidy and well-kept, others shabby, but all offering some essential goods or services. You simply had to know where to look.

The street was busy, though less crowded than Seventh Street, where Meade had exited the streetcar. Men loitered, chatting or simply watching the world go by. The women, on the other hand, moved with purpose. Meade noticed that he was now the only white person in sight.

In the middle of the second block, Margaret stopped in front of a freshly painted storefront with a sign above it that read: "Douglass Café and Barbecue."

"'Douglass,'" Meade said, looking up. Then at her. "You spell your name with a double S?"

"Me and my whole family," she said, already amused by what she knew was coming next.

"And does that family include Frederick Douglass?"

"Yes, it does," she said. "He and my father are cousins—second cousins, third cousins, I'm not sure. But I guess that makes me a cousin, too."

Meade studied her face for any family resemblance to the famous abolitionist but saw none.

"And yes, to your next question," she added. "We see Cousin Frederick quite often. We're among the few relatives who still speak to him. He visits us regularly. Besides, he likes my dad's barbecue."

Meade backtracked slightly. "Why did the rest of the family fall out with him?"

"His wife died some time ago, and he remarried—a white woman named Helen Pitts."

"Why did that cause a rift?"

"Because she was white. His children saw the marriage as an insult to their mother. So did others in the family."

"But not your father?"

"No. He's always liked Frederick. My mother, though, wanted to join the boycott. My father might've gone along with her, except..."

"Except for what?"

"Except for me. I told her if she did that, I was moving out."

"That's pretty bold."

"Well, there was another reason some of the women in our family didn't like Helen Pitts."

"What's that?"

"She's a suffragist. A lot of women around here don't like suffrage. I'm not one of them."

"I didn't think so."

She turned toward the café door. "But I didn't bring you here to talk about family dynamics. I have something else in mind."

A bell rang as she opened the door. "The café isn't open yet. It will be in about an hour, but I can get you some coffee."

"That would be nice. Thank you."

While she disappeared into the back room, Meade took in the place—about a dozen tables, all draped with neat checkerboard cloths, chairs placed evenly, and a long counter with barstools along one wall. Behind it, the kitchen.

She returned with two steaming cups of coffee. "Please, have a seat."

"This is a wonderful place," Meade said. "Family-run, I assume?"

"All family. My parents own it. My brothers and cousins and anyone ever connected to the Douglass name works here."

She sipped her coffee, then added, "Family matters to us, Mr. Meadows. Not long ago, people like us didn't have families—not ones that stayed together. We could be sold away at any moment. Now, we can have a family and expect to keep it. We don't take that for granted."

Meade drew breath to respond, but she continued, "Like I said, that's not why I asked you here."

She leaned in slightly. "I didn't mean to eavesdrop this morning, but I overheard your conversation with Professor Watkins. I know he told you about the four students who went to Spain."

"He did."

"He told you that because he assumed you'd find out anyway, and he wanted to head you off from talking to them."

"Why wouldn't he want me to talk to them?"

"Because you might find out more than he wants you to know."

Meade said nothing. She would speak in her own time.

"My boyfriend was one of the four. Joseph Williams. The professor selected what he called his 'best' geography students for that trip."

"You didn't agree with his choice?"

"I'm a geography major too, but I didn't qualify."

"Because you're a woman."

"Because I'm a woman."

She refilled their cups and brought a tray with fresh sweet rolls.

Meade looked out the window. A framed photograph of Frederick Douglass, credited to Mathew Brady, hung between two large picture windows.

Then a broad-shouldered man entered from the kitchen. "My daughter tells me we have the famous Meade Meadows with us."

"Dennis Douglass," the man said, shaking Meade's hand. "Welcome anytime."

"Thank you, Mr. Douglass. Your daughter has been very kind."

"She knows how to talk. That's her mother's doing." He laughed and disappeared into the back.

"Joseph was more loyal to you than to Professor Watkins?"

Margaret smiled. "He told me things he wouldn't tell anyone else. That trip to Spain—it wasn't about learning Spanish. He barely improved. But he and the others were instructed to map Spain's coastline, gather data, and send daily sealed reports to the American Embassy in Madrid."

Mapping Spain's coast. Sending reports. This was espionage—academic camouflage or not.

Meade listened closely.

"They weren't allowed to keep copies. Professor Watkins gave them wax and a seal. Every day, they mailed their notes—topography, industries, transportation, conversations with locals—sealed and sent."

"And they never saw them again?"

"Never."

Meade showed her the map and the coded sheet. Her eyes widened.

"These are like what I saw in Watkins' office," she said. "Same style, same initials—SW."

"And the code?"

"Yes. That too. But I couldn't understand it."

Meade handed Margaret a photo of Lucinda.

"She may come to talk to you. You can trust her like you trust me."

Margaret nodded.

Then she paused. "There's something else I should tell you..."

23: The Mission to Spain

MEADE UNDERSTOOD IMMEDIATELY: MARGARET had just told him something she had never admitted to anyone—not her family, not even Joseph. She liked to think of herself as honest, forthright, someone who didn't keep secrets. But now she had. And not just any secret.

It made her real to Meade in a new way—not because she was deceitful, but because she trusted him enough to share it.

"So," Meade said carefully, "you believe the documents from Spain—the reports Joseph and the others sent to the American Embassy—ended up in Professor Watkins's office?"

She hesitated. "Maybe not exactly out in the open," she said slowly.

He nodded. *She looked in drawers, file cabinets—took opportunities when she could.* Meade didn't ask for details. She wasn't offering them, and she didn't need to. He understood.

"Were you able to look at all of the paperwork?"

"No. Just a few pages here and there. Honestly, I couldn't make much sense of them."

"Were they in Spanish?"

"No. English, but they were using some kind of code—something I didn't recognize."

"You never thought to take one?"

"I did think about it. But even if I had, I wouldn't have understood it. And I was always afraid Professor Watkins would notice something missing."

"You haven't told Joseph?"

"Absolutely not. He'd be furious."

Meade appreciated the significance of her trust. She had taken a risk telling him this. And now, he decided, it was time to show her something of equal weight.

"I want to show you something," he said.

He reached into his coat pocket and pulled out two thick, folded sheets of paper. Carefully, he unfolded the first one and laid it flat on the table. Margaret gasped.

"It's a map," she whispered. "A map of the Spanish coastline."

"Have you seen anything like it?"

"Yes," she said immediately. "There were maps like this in Professor Watkins's office—not this one exactly, but the same hand, the same initials. 'SW' in the corner. That's his. I'm sure of it."

Meade pulled out the second piece: a smaller page filled with strange symbols and broken lines of letters.

"A code," Margaret said.

"You recognize it?"

"It's the same format. Just like the others I saw. But I couldn't begin to decipher it."

"Would you try?"

She looked up at him. "Yes. Of course I'll try."

"What about the map? Could you identify what part of the coast it shows?"

She studied it for a moment. "That wouldn't be hard. It might take a little time, but yes—I could tell you the exact stretch of coast. The issue is, it's only a portion. Without the rest of the maps, it might not mean much."

"But you'd be willing to try?"

"Absolutely." She had already begun to roll up the map like a seasoned archivist. "And don't worry," she added. "No one will see it. I'll keep it safe."

"Good," Meade said, his tone suddenly grave. "It's important that you do."

She paused, sensing the shift in tone.

"In the next day or two, someone may come looking for you," he continued. He reached into his wallet and handed her a small photograph. "Her name is Lucinda. My sister. You can trust her completely. Tell her anything you would tell me."

Margaret took the photo and gave a slight nod.

"And talk to no one else about this—not even Joseph."

Margaret's brow furrowed slightly, but she said nothing. She understood.

A moment passed between them—quiet, thoughtful.

Then she spoke.

"There's one more thing I need to tell you."

"What is it?"

"It happened at the end of the trip. The day before they were supposed to board a steamer back to Liverpool—that's where they were catching the ship home."

Meade leaned in.

"They were in Barcelona, finishing up their notes. They'd just sealed their last packets when there was a knock on the hotel door. A Spanish federal officer was there. Polite. Professional. But firm. He said all four of them had to come to the police station."

"Were they under arrest?"

"No. At least, that's not how it was presented. Joseph said Watkins had prepared them for something like this—told them to cooperate, stay calm, and ask for the American consul if things got serious."

"Did they?"

"Yes and no. They went with the officer, were put in a room, left alone for a while. No threats, no raised voices. And then—"

"And then the consul showed up?"

"Exactly. Within an hour. Joseph said it was all very quiet. Each of them was questioned separately—just simple things. Where they had gone. Who they had met. One officer even asked Joseph if he'd had a good time."

"No accusations?"

"None. And when they returned to their hotel, nothing had been disturbed. They left for Liverpool the next morning without incident."

Meade sat back.

"But something happened."

"I don't know," Margaret admitted. "Joseph never made much of it. He acted like it was nothing—just a formality. Maybe it was. But I don't think so."

"Neither do I," Meade said quietly.

He let the whole story run through his mind. *It didn't add up. The sealed reports, the embassy, the Spanish police, the quick arrival of the American consul—it all pointed to something larger than a student field trip. Something official. Something planned.*

And that brought him to the next question.

"How was this trip paid for?" he asked.

Margaret was ready for it.

"That's the question everyone asks on campus. And no one really knows."

"What was the official story?"

"Watkins said the university had some extra funds."

"And you don't believe that?"

"Not for a second. Howard University never has extra funds for anything. Professors beg for resources all the time. Yet somehow, these four students took a seven-week trip to Spain, traveled along two coasts, and never lacked for anything."

"So what do you think?"

"I think the money came from somewhere else," she said. "Not from the university. From someone with a lot more to spend."

Meade nodded slowly. The pieces were stacking up.

When he stepped out of the Douglass Café and Barbecue a short time later, it was just after eleven. T Street had grown busier since he'd entered. At the corner, he saw a southbound streetcar and hurried to catch it. The platform looked empty at first glance, but Meade thought he caught movement at the far end, a figure turning away just as he looked up.

He stepped on board, found a seat, and sat down.

His thoughts churned. *The morning's conversation had brought him closer to the truth, but he didn't yet know how the pieces fit together.*

Behind him, several rows back, a small, dark figure in a black cape and hood took a seat, unnoticed by Meade.

24: Spain

T HE STREETCAR CARRYING MEADE south on Seventh Street came to a halt just half a block after he had boarded. Such stops and delays were common for streetcar riders—a wagon might overturn or get stuck on the tracks, a horse might freeze in place, or pedestrians might linger in the street, slowing everything down.

Meade paid no attention to the delay. His mind was elsewhere.

At the exact moment the streetcar stopped, Meade was thinking about Spain. Everything he had uncovered since investigating the admiral's death seemed to circle back to that country. The United States was not officially at war with Spain; in fact, diplomatic relations had remained relatively stable since the end of the Civil War.

But the absence of war masked growing tensions between the United States and several European nations. While America had been preoccupied with its internal conflict, other countries had expanded their imperial claims.

Spain was chief among them. Once a formidable world power, Spain had been weakened by internal strife and now clung desperately to the fading remnants of its empire.

At the heart of that empire was Cuba. While most of Latin America had declared independence, Cuba remained under Spanish control. The island had made several attempts, especially in the last decade, to free itself, only to face brutal repression in return.

More than once in the 1870s, the cold conflict between Spain and the United States had nearly turned hot.

Adding to the tension, slavery still existed in Cuba. Although the United States had abolished slavery in 1865, it expected neighboring territories to follow suit. Cuba had begun to implement a plan for emancipation, but many abolitionists in the U.S. found that progress lacking. Criticism of Spain's continued hold on slavery was widespread, even in the South.

Was the United States preparing for war with Spain? Had the Navy commissioned Professor Watkins' mapping expedition for that purpose? Was Admiral Radford in charge of the project—and was that what had gotten him killed?

The thought that the admiral had been murdered reminded Meade of the very real dangers that came with probing too deeply. He also thought of Margaret Douglass and the information she had given him. She had spoken freely—but had she put herself in danger by doing so?

These questions turned over in Meade's mind as the streetcar finally resumed its journey. It trundled along Seventh Street, stopping whenever a passenger rang the bell or whenever the driver spotted someone waiting to board.

At the corner of P Street, the bell rang and the streetcar came to a stop. The figure in the black cape and hood rose silently and stepped off. Though no sound was made, Meade felt the movement and turned just enough to catch a glimpse of the departing figure's hooded back. Once on the sidewalk, the figure walked purposefully east on P Street.

Meade could not tell if the figure was a man or woman, but

something had triggered a vague memory.

The streetcar clanged onward. Two blocks later, another bell rang.

This time, Meade himself stood, still lost in thought, and stepped off. He turned and began walking west along N Street.

25: The Diplomat

THE DIPLOMAT WALKED NORTH on Thirteenth Street and found the bench in Iowa Circle where he had been instructed to sit. A tall tree loomed behind the bench, casting light shadows in the early spring sun. It was a clear April morning—much warmer than the cold, damp nights the American seemed to prefer for their meetings.

The American had wanted yet another nighttime rendezvous in some dark alley or reeking saloon, but this time, the Diplomat had refused.

No, he had said firmly. *We meet in daylight. I want to see where I am—and who I'm dealing with.*

He was determined to catch a glimpse of the American at last. He had heard the man's voice many times but had never truly seen his face.

There was, of course, another reason. The Diplomat was growing increasingly annoyed by how often the American interrupted—or outright canceled—his romantic appointments. He had cultivated several liaisons with great care, and they were, by all accounts, going splendidly. These young women were intelligent, receptive, and in some cases, quite willing. To be summoned away from such delights by a cloaked figure with demands and threats—it was intolerable.

He was to be on the bench at 11 a.m., told not to speak or look at anyone. He would be approached.

The streets around the circle were busier than he'd anticipated. Pedestrians walked in clusters, chatting or laughing. Streetcars clanged by, and horses clopped noisily, their wagons groaning against the cobblestones.

He checked his pocket watch. The American had told him to dress simply, to blend in. Naturally, he ignored that suggestion. He was a diplomat, after all—he needed to look the part.

11:15.

These Americans prided themselves on punctuality, a trait alien to his homeland, where 11 o'clock could just as well mean three in the afternoon. No one in Madrid would blink. This American obsession with timetables was maddening.

The Diplomat shifted in his seat, trying to redirect his thoughts. The American had become increasingly demanding—more money, more promises. He had insisted on a pistol this time, along with heavier arms to be stashed in a predetermined location.

Despite the risks, the Diplomat had complied. If discovered, he would have been recalled instantly—perhaps worse. But he reminded himself: *this was in service of Spain.* The secret maps—those detailed, priceless renderings of the Spanish coastline—were believed to exist somewhere inside the U.S. Navy's command. If they were real, they would be invaluable. And his government was willing to pay.

The pistol in his coat gave him a momentary chill. *What if someone spotted it? What if I'm being watched now?*

He glanced from side to side. The neighborhood had changed dramatically since he was last posted in Washington. Where once there had been swampland and wooden shacks, now stood paved streets, a new streetcar line, and freshly built row houses, their brick facades vaguely reminiscent of Madrid.

He looked again at one of the houses near Rhode Island Avenue. *Was someone watching from the doorway?* No one stood there now. Perhaps it had only been his imagination.

"Did you bring the money?" a voice whispered behind him.

Instinctively, the Diplomat began to turn.

"Do not turn around," the voice said sharply. "I told you before—don't."

The Diplomat froze, facing forward.

"I'll ask again," the voice said, slightly louder this time. "Did you bring the money?"

"Yes," the Diplomat replied softly. "I have it here."

"And the gun?"

"I have that too."

"Good. When you leave, place them on the corner of the bench."

The Diplomat stiffened. He was not ready to be dismissed.

"I'm not leaving just yet. I want to know more. What's happening? How close are you?"

"They're working. That's all you need to know."

From the voice's direction, the Diplomat judged the American to be behind the tree—perhaps no more than five or six feet away.

"I must bring something back to my superiors," the Diplomat said. "I need details. I need assurance."

"I have a plan in place. It will be executed soon."

"Have you found the maps?"

"I'm close. Closer than ever."

The Diplomat recognized the futility of pressing further.

"What about your plan?" the voice asked now.

The escape plan.

"Yes, yes," the Diplomat said. "It's in place." It wasn't, not entirely—but that didn't matter just now.

"Then this conversation is over. Leave the items and go."

The Diplomat reached down and placed the envelope of money and the pistol at the corner of the bench. Just then, the voice spoke once more.

"You did walk, didn't you?"

The American had been explicit: the Diplomat was not to use the official embassy carriage. He was to walk—or use multiple methods of transportation—to avoid detection.

"Of course," the Diplomat replied. "Just as you instructed."

He stood and walked away.

That, too, was not entirely true. He had walked, yes—but only the last two blocks. The carriage that had brought him waited now at the corner of N Street. It was the Spanish ambassador's coach—lavishly appointed, gleaming, and unmistakable, with *Embajada de España en los Estados Unidos de América* emblazoned in gold across the side.

Normally, the ambassador used it. But today, the ambassador had discreetly left on foot—something about a private meeting at the home of a very old, very senile cabinet member whose young wife was... not so senile. Everyone in the embassy knew.

The Diplomat had seized his opportunity. After all, it wasn't every day he could ride in such luxury.

As he turned onto N Street, the Diplomat failed to notice a tall, clean-shaven young man walking west along the sidewalk. The man kept his head down and his pace steady, barely glancing at the ambassador's lavish coach.

But two blocks earlier, he had paused at a newsstand. And from there, he had followed.

Now, without breaking stride, he took in every detail—the Spanish crest, the ornate wheels, the gold-painted lettering on the side.

He passed by without a flicker of recognition.

But behind his eyes, the pieces were starting to fall into place.

His name was Meade Meadows

26: Lucinda Meadows

WHEN SHE RETURNED HOME from having dinner with her father later that evening, Lucinda Meadows found her brother seated in the most comfortable chair in his study, staring into a small fire flickering in the fireplace. Their father, Hubert, followed her into the room. He and Meade exchanged a few polite words, but the conversation was cryptic. Meade was obviously exhausted, and Hubert soon excused himself, announcing he was going upstairs to bed.

Once they heard his footsteps on the stairs, Lucinda sat down beside Meade.

"You look very weary," she said.

"I've had a very long day," he replied, though a slight smile of satisfaction played across his face.

"Have you had anything to eat?"

"Yes, I found something in the kitchen just after I got home."

After walking along N Street, he had caught another streetcar into town and gone to the offices of *The Washington Beacon*. As one of the paper's star reporters, he was free to come and go as he pleased, as long as his editors were kept informed of his whereabouts.

At some point during the afternoon, his editor, George Callahan, stopped by his desk.

"I understand you've been asking around with your Navy sources about the admiral," Callahan said. "Have you made any progress? Found anything out?"

Meade gave him vague responses, offering just enough to seem cooperative but withholding specifics. In other circumstances, and with other stories, Callahan might have pressed harder. But not this time. Surprisingly, he seemed satisfied.

"You might want to speak to Commander Tower before you go much further," Callahan added casually. But Meade detected something in his tone that was anything but casual.

I'll follow up on that tomorrow, Meade had thought. He made a mental note, then returned to his writing, working steadily through the afternoon and into the early evening. By the time he noticed, the newsroom had emptied. Around 7 o'clock, he realized he was alone.

Not long after, he left the building and walked the few blocks home to Connecticut Avenue in the gathering twilight.

Lucinda noticed an empty cup on the table next to his chair. "Would you like some more?" she asked. "I think I'll make a pot."

Meade said he'd very much like another cup. He had been sitting quietly for nearly an hour, but Lucinda's presence had enlivened him. He had much to tell her and had been looking forward to it.

Moments later, she returned with a tray containing a fresh pot of tea, slices of bread, and some cake. She poured herself a cup and sat down in a chair near him.

"I'm sorry I didn't see you this morning before you left," she said. "Papa and I had plans to go to dinner this evening. I had wanted you to come along."

"I don't know that it would have made for a very pleasant evening," Meade said.

Lucinda brushed off the remark. "You and Papa argue too much. You're both too strong-willed—and too stubborn—to see that you're usually trying to do each other some good. You would've been interested in what he had to say tonight."

"Oh really?" Meade said. "And what was that?"

Lucinda shook her head. "We won't get into that just now. I want to hear what you've been up to."

She took his cup and filled it with fresh tea, then handed him a piece of cake on a small plate.

"Now, brother," she said, "every detail you can remember—I want to hear it all."

Meade obliged, beginning with his trip the day before to find Benny MacBain.

"Benny wasn't hard to find. Once I bought him a couple of beers, he was very congenial and talkative." Meade recounted most of what Benny, the old sailor and friend of Watkins, had told him.

"The place where you found him—that's a pretty rough part of Annapolis, isn't it?"

"Well, it wasn't the Imperial Hotel, but it was okay." He said it lightly, hoping to ease any concern Lucinda might have about his safety. She had a protective streak—sometimes bordering on over-protectiveness.

Meade then described his streetcar ride to the Howard University campus and his encounter in Professor Sylvester Watkins's outer office.

"I'll tell you more about her in a minute," he said. Meade started relaying what Watkins had told him, but Lucinda interrupted.

"Describe the office first," she said. "Everything you can remember."

"It was a bit of a mess—maps, books, charts everywhere."

"Did it look like he was working on anything in particular?"

"Yes, now that you mention it. He had some maps and charts laid out. Looked like he was filling them in with navigational data."

Lucinda paused in thought. "Okay, go on. What did he say?"

Meade said that Watkins had confirmed working on a set of charts for the Navy, mapping the coast of Spain, and that he had sent four students to gather information last fall. "Beyond that, he wouldn't say much. He told me he was saving me the trouble of tracking the students down. I didn't realize it at the time, but that was significant."

"Well, I'll tell you why in a minute," Lucinda said.

Meade finished describing the interview and said that he'd left the office frustrated. "I could tell he was holding something back, and it bothered me that I couldn't get it out of him."

He then told her about the sealed note he found pinned to the door on his way out, with instructions to board a streetcar.

"That came from the girl in the outer office, didn't it?" Lucinda asked.

She smiled. *Lucky guess.*

Meade knew better. Lucinda's guesses were rarely luck.

"And she was waiting at the streetcar stop when you got off?"

"Exactly. Her name is Margaret Douglass. She asked me to walk with her down T Street to the Douglass Café and Barbecue."

"You mean she's related to Frederick Douglass?"

Meade stared at her. "How did you know that?"

"The Douglass family is pretty well known in certain circles here. There's been some controversy, since Frederick Douglass married a white woman," Lucinda said.

"That's what Margaret said. But how do you know all this?"

Lucinda looked at him with gentle pity. "Dear, dear brother—you think being a big-time newspaper reporter means you know everything going on in this city. But there's plenty you'll never hear about in the *Beacon* newsroom. Especially when it involves families like the Douglasses. They're Black, and many white people still think that means they don't count."

Meade felt mildly chastised—but a scolding from Lucinda always came with such a soft touch that he almost welcomed it. Meade knew from long experience that his sister knew things he didn't know and could see things clearly before they ever materialized in front of him. He had grown smart enough never to take offense at anything she said.

"You never cease to amaze me, my dear sister."

She took the compliment without comment, as she usually did. "So what did Margaret Douglass have to tell you?"

Meade said that Margaret believed Watkins had told him about the Spain trip to keep him from seeking out the students directly. One of those students was her boyfriend. Though sworn to secrecy, he had told her much of what happened—how they wrote detailed nightly reports, sealed them, and mailed them to the U.S. embassy in Madrid every morning.

"And then I asked if she had seen any of those reports."

Lucinda leaned in. "And she said...?"

"She said yes. She'd been in Watkins's office when he wasn't there and had gone looking for them."

"That's risky. Why take the chance?"

"She respects Watkins, but she thinks the students deserve more credit. And," Meade added, "I think she resents that only men were chosen for the trip."

"A feminist," Lucinda said. "Probably a suffragist too."

She's probably right again, Meade thought.

Meade told her that he had shown Margaret the map and coded paper he had taken from the admiral's study, and she confirmed that they looked similar to papers in Watkins's office.

"She said she could probably figure out more if she had more time to study them, so I left them with her."

Lucinda considered this. "I think that was a good idea."

"Yes, but I'm not sure you'll approve of what I did next."

"What was that?"

"I told her you'd come visit in the next day or two, to talk about what she'd found."

Lucinda thought a moment. "I'd be happy to. Margaret sounds like someone I'd like to meet."

Meade was about to tell her what happened the rest of that morning when a loud knock startled them both.

They exchanged glances, then another knock rang out. Meade leapt from his chair like a greyhound from the gate and dashed into the hall. When he grabbed the door handle, he felt resistance from the other side. With a sharp tug—then another—he forced it open on the third pull.

A string had been tied to the outside door handle and then to a front bush. It hadn't locked the door completely, just enough to delay anyone answering.

Meade stepped outside and looked up and down Connecticut Avenue. It was nearly 11 p.m. The street was empty.

Frustrated, he stepped forward—then spotted a folded piece of paper on the doorstep. He picked it up and looked around again.

Still no one.

He turned and walked slowly back inside. Lucinda stood just beyond the open door.

"What's that?"

He glanced down, almost having forgotten the note in his hand. "Whoever was just here must have left this."

Back in the light, Meade unfolded the paper. It read:

Pleese come quick, have much informashun. Meet me at Townhouse Sal. Burley O.

Lucinda saw the widened look in his eyes.

"It's Burley," Meade said. "He must be in some kind of trouble. I need to get there quick."

Before she could stop him, he dashed to his study for his coat. As he re-entered the hallway, Lucinda caught him in a quick hug.

"Be careful," she said. "Be very careful."

27: The Note

Lucinda went to the open door and watched as Meade hurried down Connecticut Avenue. The distance from their house to the **Townhall Saloon** on E Street wasn't great, but it was too far for him to run at full speed. She hoped he might still be able to find a hack or a hansom cab.

That was her hope. But Lucinda remembered the warnings Meade had received when he first began looking into the admiral's death. It was a dangerous thing to pursue, he'd been told—after all, if the admiral had indeed been murdered, whoever had done it would likely have no compunction about killing again.

As the moments passed and she remained alone, Lucinda wished more and more that Meade hadn't been so hasty. They should have taken at least a moment to think it through, she told herself. *I should have insisted.*

Lost in self-admonishment, she turned back into the hallway—and saw the note lying on the floor. She picked it up, unfolded it, and read it carefully.

What has Burley O'Malley gotten himself into? she thought.

She had never met Burley O'Malley, though she had seen him from a distance. Based on what Meade had said, and what she herself had observed, she believed Burley was the kind of man who could handle himself in just about any situation. Why, then, would he send an urgent note demanding Meade's help?

And why a note?

If it had come by messenger—as it obviously had—why had the messenger fled so quickly? Why hadn't he stayed to explain? And why had the door been tied with string, as if to prevent them from seeing who had delivered it?

Lucinda looked at the note again. Something about it struck her as odd.

She hurried back into the study and began rifling through the drawers of Meade's desk. "It's got to be here somewhere," she muttered.

In the top right-hand drawer, she found it—the note Meade had received the night of the admiral's death, summoning him to the admiral's office. She spread that note out on the desk, and beside it, she laid the one that had just arrived.

Both had clearly been typed. That much was obvious. But she immediately spotted what she had been looking for: the letter E in both notes was slightly misaligned—tilted just enough to catch the eye of someone looking for it.

"These were typed on the same machine," she said aloud.

They had been sent by the same person.

But Burley O'Malley? Her mind went immediately to him, and she drew the obvious conclusion: Burley had set a trap for Meade—just like the night of the admiral's death.

A wave of fear swept through her. Meade was rushing into something he likely couldn't handle on his own—that much was certain.

But Burley? It still didn't make sense. Meade had come away from their conversations impressed—both by Burley's experience and by his sincerity. Meade could be impulsive—like dashing out the door tonight—but he was a fairly good judge of character. Had he misread Burley entirely?

And the note—its spelling was egregiously poor. That struck Lucinda as odd. Burley might not be a literary man, but something about the phrasing and the typing felt...off. She couldn't picture Burley hunched over a typewriter, pounding out a threatening note.

"Burley O'Malley didn't write this," she said aloud. "Someone else did."

And with that realization came another, more chilling thought:

Meade was in more danger than she had imagined.

28: The Assault

MEADE'S DASH THROUGH THE streets of Washington in the middle of the night tested both his body and his mind. The streets were not as deserted as he had expected, and at one point he wondered how odd it must look—a man striding, sometimes running, through the city at this hour.

The fatigue he had felt earlier in the evening was gone, replaced by the pure jolt of energy. Someone needed his help—or at least, he believed they did—and that was enough to drive him forward.

Down Connecticut Avenue he went, hoping to see an available carriage. None appeared. The streetcars had long since stopped running, or at least running regularly, so he was left with only his own two feet. When he reached K Street, he crossed into Farragut Square.

He had settled into a rhythm—a pace that allowed him to concentrate on both where he was going and why. Burley O'Malley had struck Meade from the first as reliable and sincere. That impression had only deepened during their brief follow-up conversations. He and Lucinda had even discussed Burley; she, too, had seemed inclined to trust him.

So why would Burley summon me in such a desperate, almost panicked fashion?

The question followed him as he pressed forward.

Near Lafayette Square, the streets grew more populated again. A few horse-drawn carriages sped past—already occupied. An empty one was parked outside a bar facing the square, but Meade saw no sign of the driver. *He's probably inside,* Meade thought. *And drunk. I don't have time to pull him out.*

He cut diagonally through the square, crossed Executive Avenue, and passed in front of the White House. He broke into a full sprint—only a few blocks now stood between him and the **Townhall Saloon**.

But this part of town posed its own problems. There were always people on the streets, day or night. Most of them weren't moving with purpose. Many were loitering—some looking for a drink, others for mischief.

Several women spotted him from a distance and moved to intercept him, but Meade's sprint sent them scattering.

Finally, he reached the street and spotted the **Townhall Saloon** two blocks away.

He passed the Imperial Hotel—and came to an abrupt stop.

Three large men blocked his path.

They had emerged from the alley between the hotel and the next row of shops. Standing shoulder to shoulder, they glared at him. All three wore dark, wide-brimmed hats that cast shadows over their faces. Their clothes were rough and bore the marks of manual labor—sailors, most likely, though with no rank or insignia.

"You've come far enough," said the man in the middle.

Two of them were larger than Meade; the third, who had spoken, was about his size.

Meade stopped cold.

He could try to turn and run. He was sure he could outrun

them—they didn't look nimble. But something in him resisted retreat.

I'm not going back, he thought. *I'm going forward.*

He paused. Let his shoulders drop. Made fear register on his face.

Then, in one sudden motion, he lunged forward—aiming straight for the man in the center.

It was a mistake.

The man sidestepped him, and one of the others slammed a shoulder into Meade's side. He hit the ground hard. A pair of boots struck his ribs. He tried to roll, but it was too late—they were dragging him into the alley.

Out of view of the street, the kicks resumed. One man dropped to his knees and pounded Meade's back with both fists. Meade curled into a tight ball, protecting what he could.

Then, just as suddenly, the blows stopped.

"Consider this a message, Meadows," said the one who had spoken earlier. "Ask another question about the admiral's death, and things won't go as well for you next time."

A fist struck Meade's face. More kicks followed.

Then came a sharp whistle and a voice—loud and commanding.

"Stop!"

The attackers vanished. Their boots slapped against the pavement as they fled.

Meade lay in the dirt. Pain throbbed through his ribs, his limbs, his face. He couldn't yet move—but he would.

"Sir? Sir, are you hurt?"

A woman's voice.

She knelt beside him, her hand on his shoulder, gently touching his face.

Meade looked up, dazed. He didn't recognize her.

"Tell me where you're hurt."

He couldn't answer. His ribs ached, his arms burned. All he knew was that he needed to stand. *If they come back, I have to be on my feet.*

He tried to push himself up, but couldn't.

"I'm going to help you," she said. "There's a hotel right here. We need to get you inside."

She shifted beside him, wedging herself under his arm. Slowly, they rose.

Meade stumbled forward, leaning heavily on her. Together, they reached the sidewalk. The streetlamps were bright enough to reveal her face.

Dark hair. Large, expressive eyes. A warm, firm grip.

She was very short—but very strong.

"This way, sir," she said, leading him toward the hotel entrance just off the sidewalk.

More light shone on her face as they approached the door.

And suddenly, Meade knew exactly who she was.

She's the grieving woman from the back pew at Admiral Radford's funeral.

29: Lucinda Meadows

T HE CONVENTIONS OF THE time argued strongly against
what Lucinda was contemplating. Single white women of her
class and station did not venture out onto the streets of Washington,
D.C., at night. Women on the street after dark were considered
unsafe—vulnerable to all manner of evil and evildoers. Even in daylight, women like Lucinda, unaccompanied and outdoors, were rare.
At night, they were unthinkable.

More than that, women seen alone after sunset quickly earned
a label—one whispered through the parlors and drawing rooms
of Washington at the speed of a spring breeze. Such words, once
spoken, became permanent. They filtered upward through the social
strata, reaching the ears of the wealthy and influential.

Lucinda met and dismissed all those arguments with one
thought: *Meade is headed for trouble, and someone needs to help him.*

She briefly considered waking her father. He would certainly be
willing—eager, even. Hubert Meadows was never one to back down
from a challenge.

But he would be slow. Getting him up and out the door would
take time—and Lucinda had none to spare.

In the cloakroom at the end of the front hallway, she grabbed a
dark, lightweight overcoat and flung it around her shoulders. She

buttoned the top, then pulled a dark blue scarf—a bit larger than necessary—around her head. Thus armed, she slipped out the door, closing it softly behind her so as not to wake her father. An instant later, she was on Connecticut Avenue, taking the same route into the city that Meade had traveled only minutes before.

The street was almost empty. One or two pedestrians hurried past, but no one gave her a second glance. Her long skirts and dark cloak helped conceal her, and she lifted the hem just enough to free her stride. Urgency propelled her forward, and any stares she might have attracted went unnoticed.

In truth, few noticed her at all. Most of those out at this hour were revelers—some drunk, some laughing, many wandering—but all too preoccupied to care about a lone woman striding with purpose.

Like Meade, she scanned for a carriage to hail as she passed through Farragut Square. None appeared.

At Lafayette Square, however, she spotted one. It was the same carriage Meade had seen earlier, parked in front of a small bar within view of the President's House. As she approached, a man emerged from the bar to check on his horse.

"Sir, are you the driver of this carriage?" she asked.

"Yes, madam," he said. "But I went off duty an hour ago, and I'm well on my way to getting drunk. Thank you very much. Good night, madam."

His tone and manner made clear that he took pleasure in refusing his services to a beautiful young woman—perhaps for the first time that day. He turned to re-enter the bar.

"That's a shame," Lucinda said loudly. "The man who could give me a ride right now will not have to work for the next two days. But sir, you're off duty, so I cannot ask."

She turned and began to walk away.

It took him five seconds to register what she had said—and one second to shout: "Wait! I'm on duty!"

Lucinda turned back, handed him a ten-dollar bill, and said, "Take me to E Street. Do not slow down for anything or anyone."

The driver obeyed, and the trip to E Street took five minutes less than it would have on foot. When they arrived in front of the Imperial Hotel, she said, "Wait here until I return," in a tone that allowed no debate.

She stepped out and looked down the dimly lit sidewalk. The street was alive with people—some loitering, others talking or laughing, a few clearly intoxicated. The air was thick with the smells of alcohol, cigar smoke, and unwashed bodies. Music drifted from nearby saloons. As she scanned the scene, she spotted several unaccompanied women—women whose business it was to be on E Street at this hour.

Lucinda didn't hesitate. She approached the nearest one.

"Excuse me," she said. "I'm looking for someone." She began to describe Meade.

"Get lost, lady," the woman sneered. "This is my section. Go find your own corner." She turned to walk away.

Lucinda grabbed her arm with surprising force and spun her back around. The woman's face flushed with anger—until Lucinda raised a five-dollar bill in front of her eyes.

"Are you going to tell me what I want to know," Lucinda said coolly, "or should I ask the girl across the street?"

After Lucinda gave a quick description—"Tall, heavy overcoat, full head of hair, handsome, heading to the **Townhall Saloon**"—the woman snatched the bill, but Lucinda kept hold of her arm.

"Yeah, honey, I saw him just a few minutes ago. He got to the corner by the hotel there, and some big lugs grabbed him. Dragged him into the alley. That's all I know." She yanked her arm away and crossed the street.

The woman's words chilled Lucinda. Without hesitation, she started toward the alley.

Just then, Meade appeared.

Even in the dim light, she could tell he was hurt—limping badly, supported by a small, dark-haired woman in a hooded cloak. Meade stopped in the doorway of the hotel and turned his head slightly. As if sensing her, his eyes found Lucinda at once.

Her first instinct was to call out and run to him. But before she could, he looked at her, gave a subtle shake of the head, and turned back to the woman who was helping him. Together, they disappeared into the hotel.

Lucinda stood motionless, realization dawning.

This was the woman Meade had seen at Admiral Radford's funeral.

30: The Imperial Hotel

THE IMPERIAL HOTEL OFFERED everything that could be considered elegant in Washington, D.C., hospitality. Its furnishings were tasteful but not gaudy. The wood-paneled walls and polished registration desk gleamed. Though European in design, the furniture was American-made—and proudly advertised as such.

Still, the Imperial suffered not from its reputation, but from its location and competition. The Willard Hotel, only a half block away, was closer to the Treasury and the President's House. Its furnishings were a little shabbier—though still refined—but the Willard wasn't located on Washington's "row."

To call the Imperial a "rum hotel" was unfair—rum really started a block away—but geography was everything in Washington. To compensate, the Imperial over-delivered. Its dining room served the finest meals in the city. Its bar and wine cellar had no equal in the Mid-Atlantic. And above all, its staff were known for their flawless hospitality.

That hospitality was on full display as Meade and the woman supporting him staggered through the front doors and collapsed onto one of the hotel's immaculate sofas.

"Good evening, sir. Good evening, madam. May I be of assistance?" asked a hotel clerk who appeared instantly. His voice was soft, careful not to draw the attention of others. He paid no mind to Meade's disheveled state, nor the fact that the small woman beside him was propping him up.

The woman looked up. "We need a bowl of water, some clean linen, and a bottle of whiskey."

"Right away, madam." And the clerk vanished.

With effort, the woman pulled off Meade's outer coat, rolled it up, and stuffed it beneath the sofa. That alone improved his appearance significantly—he no longer looked like he'd been crawling through an alley.

Meade, for his part, was still too dazed to think clearly. He was certain he'd seen Lucinda in the street—and that he'd signaled her not to approach—but everything beyond that was a blur. Pain radiated from his limbs and ribs, clouding his thoughts.

Was she really there? Or did I imagine it?

"Sir, how are you feeling?" the woman asked. Her voice was low and calm—deeper than most women's voices.

"I'm... I'm okay," he said, though it came out slurred.

The clerk returned with a tray holding a bowl of water, a carafe, towels, and two glasses. He set it silently on the table in front of them.

"Mr. Meadows, I thought you might need these before we get you your whiskey." Then he vanished once more.

The lobby wasn't crowded, but there were enough guests milling about that no one paid Meade or his companion much attention.

The mention of his name brought Meade back to himself.

He had been to the Imperial many times—they knew him here.

"You're Meade Meadows?" the woman asked, surprised.

She dipped a towel in the water and gently washed his face. There were cuts on his cheek and chin, but nothing serious. When she dabbed a sore spot, he winced.

The clerk reappeared, reached beneath the sofa, retrieved Meade's coat, and said, "I'll clean this off and hang it up for you." Then he vanished again.

The woman turned back to Meade. "They know you very well here," she said. "And now I know you too. You're Meade Meadows, the reporter. The one who caught President Garfield's killer."

Meade's mind had cleared just enough to deliver his standard reply.

"That's not exactly how it happened," he said. "I didn't catch anybody." His voice trailed off as he tried to gather his thoughts.

The woman poured him a glass of water and handed it over. He took a sip. The cool water hit his tongue and seemed to clear a fog from his mind.

"You're the woman I saw at Admiral Radford's funeral," he said.

She looked at him, hesitating before answering.

But before she could speak, another voice interrupted.

"Your whiskey, sir. Will there be anything else?"

Meade turned toward the voice.

Lucinda.

She wore the uniform of a hotel staff member and carried a tray with a bottle of whiskey and two glasses. She looked directly at Meade—and gave him the faintest shake of the head.

Lucinda? What is she doing here? How had she gotten into that uniform so fast?

"Lu—" he began, but she silenced him with her eyes.

"No," he said quickly. "Nothing else. Thank you."

31: Catherine Parrish

"MY NAME IS CATHERINE Parrish," she said, her voice soft and low, with an accent that hinted at a drawl. Not Deep South—more like Mid-Atlantic.

Meade and Catherine had been sitting in the lobby of the Imperial Hotel, virtually unnoticed by other guests and visitors, for about twenty minutes. Meade had been trying to clear his head and recover from the pain in his ribs left by his three assailants.

This was the third time Catherine had spoken her name.

Meade held in his hand his second glass of whiskey. His head was finally beginning to clear, and his thoughts were starting to make sense. The familiar surroundings of the hotel helped restore his balance. The lobby had quieted considerably since they entered—or maybe it was just his ears that had finally stopped buzzing.

"It's a good thing I came along when I did," she said. "Those men meant to do you some harm."

Meade tried to reconstruct what had happened over the last fifteen to twenty minutes. He kept assembling a sequence of events that made sense—but he wasn't quite there yet.

Yes, it was good that she had come along when she did. Very good. Very propitious. The timing was almost perfect. What if she had been two or three minutes later? What would have happened then?

"Why did you come along when you did?" he asked. "This isn't a good time—or place—for someone to be out alone at night."

She sat back on the sofa, holding her whiskey glass, which still contained a drinkable amount. She stared into it for a moment, then leaned forward and lowered her voice.

"I have to tell you," she began, "it's not by chance that I'm here tonight."

"What do you mean?"

Catherine took a deep breath and began. Her whole manner conveyed a reluctance to reveal herself.

"I'm a clerk in the Navy Department. I work mostly in the supplies office down at the Navy Yard, but sometimes I'm sent to other Navy offices when they need someone who can add and subtract."

"And not everyone in the Navy can do that?"

She laughed. "Sometimes it seems that way." Her body relaxed slightly. She seemed more comfortable now. "Anyway, it's well known around the Navy offices that Washington's most famous news reporter has been asking questions about Admiral Radford's death. Most people I hear say it was suicide, but your questions—at least the way people talk about them—suggest you don't believe that. That you think something else is going on."

"That's a fair assessment."

"I don't know anything for sure, but I do know there are people who are not happy with what you're doing. And when I say *not happy*, I'm understating."

"Why is that?"

"I'm not entirely sure," she said. "People tend to forget about me. I don't say much—I just do my job. And when people forget about you, they sometimes say things they shouldn't."

"What kind of things?"

"Things like... you're turning over rocks that certain people—powerful people—don't want disturbed."

"And do you know what's under those rocks?"

She shook her head. "Oh no, I don't know that." She said it quickly. *Maybe too quickly.* For someone who claimed ignorance, she seemed to know quite a bit.

"But you have an idea."

She hesitated. "Yes, maybe I do. Not a clear idea. But the admiral. .. well, he was involved in secret operations. And even though he was well respected—" She cut herself off. "I'm not making much sense, am I?"

Meade smiled but stayed silent. He didn't want her to stop.

"Well, anyway," she continued, "I came here tonight because I overheard some of the men talking down at the Navy Yard this afternoon. I didn't hear much, but I did hear that this was the night you needed to be warned off. That you were going to be taught a lesson."

Meade processed that. "So you followed them?"

"Yes. I sometimes work late, and I pretended that I had something to finish tonight. The men left the Navy Yard and headed to the Townhouse Saloon. I waited in an alley across the street, hoping to see you and warn you. But the crowd made it hard. I didn't see you until just before they grabbed you."

Meade thought about what she said. The men who'd attacked him hadn't come out of the Townhouse Saloon—they'd emerged from the alley beside the Imperial Hotel. The saloon was a block and a half farther down E Street.

Did she get confused—or was she trying to place herself farther from the scene?

Perhaps she noticed his scrutiny. She quickly added, "Some people in the Navy think you've come across something important—something that could explain the admiral's death. That's probably why you were attacked."

Was she trying to find out what I know? Meade's instincts told him to be careful.

"You're probably right," he said noncommittally.

He studied her closely. She was petite, with a round face and large gray eyes. Her high cheekbones and well-proportioned features gave her a striking appearance. Despite describing herself as a lowly clerk, she exuded quiet intelligence and confidence.

Just then, Meade heard Lucinda's voice: "May I pour you another drink, sir?" Her tone was her best imitation of hotel staff—equal parts officious and obsequious.

Meade didn't look up. He simply held out his glass and said, "Yes, thank you."

Catherine looked up at Lucinda briefly but gave no indication that she recognized her as anyone other than a hotel employee.

Unbeknownst to either of them, Lucinda had been standing behind a nearby pillar for several minutes, close enough to hear nearly the entire conversation.

Meade looked down at his glass, then back at Catherine. "Well then," he said, "I suppose I have you to thank for not being more seriously injured."

"I just wish I'd reached you before they started swinging."

They both sipped their drinks. Noticing that the bottle was nearly empty, Meade asked, "Shall I order another?"

"Oh no," she said quickly. "I rarely drink. But this whiskey is very good."

Lucinda reappeared, still in her role. "Madam," she said, "may I pour you another?"

Catherine held out her glass, and Lucinda emptied the last of the bottle into it. "Thank you," she said.

Lucinda turned to Meade. "Sir, would you like another bottle?"

Meade hesitated. "No, thank you."

For a brief moment, Meade considered Lucinda. *How many times has she backed me up like this—quietly, cleverly, without being asked? She can be exhausting with all her questions, but I've learned to listen.*

He turned back to Catherine.

"You were at the admiral's funeral." It was a statement and a question.

"Yes, yes I was." She spoke slowly, deliberately.

"And you seemed very upset," he said. "Why?"

Catherine stared at the floor. She started to speak, stopped, then took a deep breath.

"That's a long story," she said.

32: Burley O'Malley

THE SURVEILLANCE COMMANDER NATHAN Tower had placed on the Spanish ambassador over the last seven weeks had produced little of value. They now knew for certain that the ambassador was conducting a semi-public affair with the wife of the Postmaster General—but that was hardly a secret. The Postmaster General, a senile fool, had married a beautiful widow more than thirty years his junior. The Spanish ambassador fancied himself a romantic hero, but Tower saw little more than vanity.

He had used his limited resources to track the ambassador and his lover, but both leads had turned out to be dead ends. The espionage Nathan was certain was flowing from the Spanish embassy had to be coming from someone else. He had suspects, but no solid leads.

Tower sat lost in these thoughts in a safe house on C Street. Burley O'Malley had sent word less than thirty minutes earlier requesting a meeting. Rather than meet at his office—where prying eyes and ears might still linger—Nathan preferred the house on C Street for its discretion.

Tower had learned patience, especially from his love of baseball. The game's slow rhythm, sudden bursts of action, and unexpected reversals had taught him that situations could change in a moment. You could be down three runs and then take the lead with one swing.

Be ready for the moment, he reminded himself.

Burley O'Malley appeared silently in the upstairs doorway. Tower hadn't heard a sound.

"Cap'n."

"Burley."

That was greeting enough. Burley sat across from Nathan at a small table with a pitcher of beer between them. Nathan had already poured a glass and drunk half.

"Where were you tonight, Burley?"

Burley took a sip of beer. "Started out watching Meade's house, like you said. Was just about to call it a night when a little kid showed up, banging on the front door, tying the handle with string, and then running off."

"Did you get a good look at him?"

"Just a kid. Probably paid a nickel to deliver the note and vanish." Burley took another drink.

"Meade opened the door, ran into the street, but the kid was long gone. Then he saw the note. He and his sister read it, and a second later, he comes flying out of the house and heads south down Connecticut. He was moving fast—I had trouble keeping up."

"But you managed."

Burley grinned. "Sort of. Found a carriage parked near Farragut Square. Driver was inside, getting drunk, so I figured a good citizen ought to lend a hand to his federal government."

"In other words, you stole it."

"I prefer *borrowed*," Burley said, grinning.

"You caught up with Meade?"

"Just as he turned onto E Street. The street was busy, but he didn't slow down. Then he stopped—three big guys were blocking his way near the Imperial Hotel. Looked like Navy men, but I didn't recognize them."

"And Meade wasn't going to stop."

"No sir. He went straight at them. Didn't go well for him."

"They dragged him into an alley?"

"Yep. I couldn't see much. Wasn't sure if I should jump in, but I was about to when—bam—this woman shows up with a whistle. Yells at them to stop. By the time I got close, the three were gone, and she was helping Meade up."

"Did you get a good look at her?"

"A little. Small, dark-haired, wore a black hood. Couldn't see much. But she helped him into the Imperial."

"You followed them?"

"Watched through the window. They sat on a sofa. Then the staff brought them towels, water. Treated them like royalty."

"They do that well at the Imperial."

"Then I tried to sneak inside. Was just getting close enough to maybe hear something—and bam—Lucinda shows up."

"Lucinda Meadows?"

"The very one. Pretending to be hotel staff. Pouring drinks, playing along. Meade didn't acknowledge her."

"And she was the one who ended up listening?"

"Yep. Took the best spot near them. I backed off."

Nathan leaned back.

"And then you sent word to me."

"Found a kid outside. Cost me fifty cents."

"He charged me another fifty," Nathan said with a chuckle. "Said you promised him a dollar."

Burley grinned. "Got anything to eat? I'm gonna get scurvy."

"Kitchen's downstairs," Nathan said. "And what you saw tonight was useful. Raises questions."

"Questions are your department, Cap'n. I just report what I see."

"Understood."

Burley headed for the food. Nathan remained seated, sorting through the evening's revelations.

Why had Meade rushed to E Street? Who were the attackers? Who was the woman? And what the hell was Lucinda doing there?

But two questions overrode the rest:

Who was trying to steal the Spanish maps—and where, exactly, were they?

The admiral hadn't worried about their location. But the admiral was dead.

Nathan rose and walked across the room to a corner where a telephone stood.

He picked it up, called for an operator, and waited to be connected.

"Hubert, this is Tower. I think it's time we got together."

33: The Douglass Café and Barbecue

"LET ME TELL YOU something about your father."

Commander Nathan Tower sat at one of the tables in the Douglass Café and Barbecue on T Street, dressed in his usual business suit instead of his Navy uniform. It was a chilly April day—the second since Meade Meadows had been assaulted in the alley beside the Imperial Hotel, an incident that had led to his meeting the woman he had seen, grief-stricken, at Admiral Ezra Radford's funeral.

Across the table from Tower sat Meade Meadows and his sister, Lucinda Meadows. The restaurant was empty except for the three of them. The curtains on the windows had been drawn, and the front door was locked. A sign on the door announced that the restaurant was closed for the day.

Tower looked straight at Meade. "I know that you don't always get along with your father," he said. "I understand that. I've known your father for many years—he can be a difficult man."

Meade held Tower's gaze but said nothing, hoping his face hadn't betrayed any reaction.

Tower then turned to Lucinda. "I understand that you have a

somewhat better relationship with your father."

Lucinda thought for a moment, then said matter-of-factly, "I am eager to hear what you have to tell us about Papa."

Tower sensed the siblings' skepticism. His tone carried a note of admiration, particularly for Lucinda, whose poise impressed him.

"As you know," Tower continued, "your father was one of the most outspoken Unionists in Nashville at the beginning of the Civil War. You were just children at the time, but I'm sure you understand that his views put his business, his freedom, and his life in danger."

"We are well aware of that, Commander Tower," Lucinda said.

"What you probably don't know is that, from the very beginning of the war—especially during that first year when the Confederate Army occupied Nashville—your father was an intelligence agent for the United States Army."

"Intelligence agent?" Meade interjected.

"He was a spy," Lucinda said.

"He provided very valuable information to the Army at that time," Tower continued. "What he learned about Confederate movements helped the Union take Fort Donelson. That, in turn, meant Confederate forces could no longer hold Nashville. I've been told his intelligence was vital in making that happen."

"Did you know him then?" Meade asked.

Tower shook his head. "Yes. I was a young officer in the Navy, assigned to one of the ironclads on the Mississippi and Ohio Rivers. After the capture of Fort Donelson, we could access the Cumberland River. I steamed into Nashville a couple of times and had the opportunity to meet your father. But after that, I spent most of my time at sea."

Lucinda appeared unfazed by the revelation. "Why are you telling us this, Commander?"

"I have my reasons," he said. "One is that he's unlikely to tell you himself. He performed admirably during a national crisis. He literally put his life on the line. I doubt he'd ever speak of it—not even to the two people he holds dearest."

"We admire our father very much," Lucinda replied. "And nothing you say could change that one way or the other. I'm sure you understand. So—what are your other reasons?"

It didn't surprise Meade that the conversation had centered on his father. Hubert had always cast a long shadow in his life. Only after establishing himself in Washington as a respected news reporter had Meade begun to feel somewhat free of his father's influence. But he had never been completely free—Hubert knew too many people, had made too many friends, and done too many favors. Commander Tower, Meade realized, was simply another admirer in a long line.

In fact, Hubert was the reason he and Lucinda were sitting here at all. After the unsettling events at the Imperial Hotel, Hubert had insisted that they meet with Commander Tower—and had brought them here himself. *One question kept running through Meade's mind: Why this place in particular? It was, after all, where he had met Margaret Douglass. Coincidence? Or something more?*

Tower turned toward Lucinda. "Let me tell you who I am. I work in the Office of Naval Intelligence. I'm not the commanding officer—far from it—but I'm in charge of assigning naval attachés to foreign embassies. I also train those attachés and process some of the information they send back."

"I have a feeling," Lucinda said, "that you do much more than that. And I also suspect my father is involved."

"You're correct on both counts, Miss Meadows. What I described are my official duties."

"Another feeling I have," Lucinda said, "is that you should call me Lucinda."

Tower smiled in assent.

"Americans," he said, leaning back a little, "tend to be naive about how the world works. We think that if we're not shooting at another country's soldiers, we must be at peace. And that everyone likes us. That they take our good intentions at face value."

"Where is this going, Commander?" Meade asked, impatiently.

Tower raised a calming hand. "I know it sounds like I'm beating around the bush, but I have a point, Meade."

"Thank you," Meade said, softening.

"My point is that as the United States grows—economically and militarily—it becomes a major power. And a major power needs a navy. Thankfully, a few people in this country—your father among them—have seen that and have pushed Congress and every administration to build a competitive Navy."

He took a breath before continuing.

"And a competitive Navy needs intelligence. It needs an intelligence system. And I'll use words that I hope won't shock you: that system must include espionage and counterespionage."

"I still don't see what this has to do with us," Meade said.

"Well," Tower replied, "your father, in addition to being a Civil War hero, is also a modern-day patriot who understands the need for intelligence gathering and supports our efforts strongly."

Lucinda leaned forward. "When you say 'supports,' what exactly do you mean?"

"I can't tell you everything," Tower said. "But I can say that your father is closely aligned with our mission."

"And us?" Meade asked. "How do we fit in?"

"Until a few days ago, you didn't. But when the admiral died—and when his widow asked you to investigate—you stepped directly into the middle of one of our operations."

"In other words," Lucinda said, "without intending to, we became spies."

"And what operation is that?" Meade asked.

Tower explained: Over the past few years, tensions between the U.S. and foreign powers had grown—particularly with Spain. Desperate to hold on to Cuba, Spain had become increasingly aggressive. The U.S., meanwhile, was preparing for a potential conflict. One aspect of that preparation involved mapping the Spanish coastline.

Admiral Ezra Radford had overseen the project. Professor Sylvester Watkins had been commissioned to lead the mapping team. He had sent students to Spain to gather coastal data.

"And your role?" Meade asked.

"Initially, I wasn't involved," Tower replied. "But when I learned the team was going to Spain, I saw an opportunity. One of those students was working not only for Professor Watkins—but for me."

"What was he doing?" Lucinda asked.

"Alongside the mapping work, he was also making contact with individuals—potential informants."

"Informants?" they both said at once.

"Yes," Tower said. "People who could provide intelligence on Spanish military movements—and who, in the event of war, could help U.S. forces."

"In other words, traitors," Meade said.

Tower gave a slight shrug. "Or freedom fighters. Depends on your perspective."

"And you pay them?" Meade asked.

"As I said—this is how the world works."

"Where do you get the money?"

Tower raised a hand. "We've gone far enough down that road—for now."

He explained that Watkins's team had returned with highly detailed, extraordinarily accurate maps—possibly the best ever produced of any coastline. That made the maps incredibly valuable.

"But only if other countries know they exist," Meade said.

"Exactly," Tower nodded. "I wanted this project kept secret. But word leaked. And Spain, unsurprisingly, is now desperate to obtain them."

"How do you know that?" Lucinda asked. "Surely not from your 'freedom fighters.'"

Tower's eyes lit with admiration. "No. That intel comes from higher up. We have sources in Madrid—people inside the government."

"Inside the Spanish government?" she asked.

Tower nodded. "Yes. And they've confirmed that stealing those maps is now a top priority."

"Well then," Meade said, "just lock them up and don't let anyone near them."

"I wish it were that simple," Tower said. "But we don't know where the maps are. Admiral Radford took personal charge of them, and since his death, no one has been able to locate them."

Silence followed.

That, Meade said, *is quite a complication.*

"Yes," Tower said. "And that's why I need your help."

34: The Diplomat

THE DIPLOMAT PICKED HIS way through the shadows beneath the bleachers of Seventh Street Athletic Park. Though it was noon, the April sky was overcast and gray. Glowering clouds blocked the sun, and under the stands, it might as well have been midnight.

Americans had fallen in love with a game they called baseball. The Diplomat had no idea what it entailed—and no interest. Apparently, there was a game today. He could hear the crowd arriving.

But beneath the bleachers, no one saw or heard him.

He reached the place where the American had told him to wait.

He had requested this meeting. The American had chosen the place.

At the beginning, this operation had seemed so easy. Pay an agent—presumably someone inside the U.S. Navy. Get the maps. Deliver a victory for his government.

But by the time he'd taken over—after battling through bureaucratic obstacles—a new figure had appeared. The American. At first, he thought she was a mere courier. He now knew better.

The American was in charge, demanding more money. He had resisted. He'd wanted proof. When none was provided, he began investigating. His agents scoured the bars of Washington and Baltimore. They heard whispers—of a cabal of second-generation Confederates. And rumors that a woman was leading them.

His superiors had pressured him to cooperate. *Pay her*, they said. *Whatever the price.* If he were in charge, he would have held out.

Now, here he was. In a dark place. With no maps. Just promises.

He reached into his coat. No money. Just a gun. Loaded. He had no intention of using it. It was a prop, if needed.

This had gone on long enough.

"I'm here," the American hissed, her voice just audible over the crowd above.

Yes, definitely a woman's voice. Irritated. Assertive.

The Diplomat reached for the gun again.

He had one card left to play.

He turned to see the face.

"Don't turn—"

Too late. He faced her squarely. She was shorter than he expected. The hood had made her seem taller. Even in the dim light, he could tell—she was small. *Could she really be running a spy ring?*

He reached for her hood.

She slapped his hand away, lunged slightly. He stepped back. His hand stayed on the gun.

She stopped. Composed herself.

"Don't touch," she said.

He steadied himself. "The maps. Where are they?"

"You'll know when I have them," she said coolly. "Be patient."

The time for patience is over, he snapped, motioning with the pistol. "Take that hood off."

She paused. Then slowly, deliberately, pulled back her hood.

"Curiosity satisfied?" she asked.

This wasn't about curiosity—it was about control.

"What is your name?"

A beat passed.

"My name is Catherine Parrish," she said.

Catherine Parrish? Was that the name I had heard?

He studied her face. High cheekbones. Sharp eyes. A small mole above her lip. Not beautiful. Not ugly. Plain. Easily forgettable.

"Where are the maps?"

"I don't know," she said. "I'm working on it."

Not the answer he wanted. But the one he expected.

"We need those maps," he said. "Our government and Navy are asking questions."

"I'm close," she replied.

"You have one week."

"One week?"

"A ship leaves Baltimore in seven days. If the maps are not aboard, your chances of escape drop dramatically."

"I have a plan. It's already in motion."

"Does that plan involve your journalist?"

"You don't need to know that."

"No. I don't. But I do need the maps."

He stepped closer. "We've paid you everything you asked for. If you and your Confederates don't deliver, there are people in the American government who would be very interested in what you've been doing."

It was a bluff. But he placed it on the table.

Then he turned and disappeared into the light.

Catherine stood there in the dark, momentarily stunned.

He used the word *Confederates.*

That wasn't an accident. And it meant trouble.

She watched as he vanished into the crowd.

A cold hatred began to grow in her.

Just then, a roar erupted from the field above. Something had happened in the baseball game.

And no one had any idea what had just happened beneath it.

35: The Second Generation

"**S**HE REALLY DIDN'T TELL me much that I thought was significant or even very interesting."

Meade was recounting his conversation from a day and a half earlier with Catherine Parrish—the woman he had noticed at Admiral Radford's funeral and who had come to his aid after he was attacked beside the Imperial Hotel.

"She talked a bit about her background," he said.

Commander Tower listened intently. "What did she say about that?"

"She mentioned that her father had fought for the Confederacy, even though their family was from somewhere up in the mountains of Maryland."

"Did she share anything about his war experiences?" Tower asked.

"Not really," Lucinda chimed in. She had been standing behind a pillar, listening to the conversation. "She said that after the war, her father never discussed his experiences and that things like the Confederacy had pretty much been forgotten."

"Did you believe her?" Tower asked Lucinda.

"No, I didn't," she replied. "There was something about her—her tone, her voice, her manner. I can't put my finger on it, but it felt like she was saying one thing while truly believing another."

Tower looked at Meade. "How did you feel about that?"

Meade shrugged. "I didn't think much about it either way. I was more interested in why she was the one person at the admiral's funeral who seemed genuinely grieved."

"Did you ask her about that?"

"Yes, and she seemed hesitant to give a straight answer. She said she met the admiral while working as a Navy clerk, visiting offices to check their books. She found him pleasant—a fatherly figure who had done her a few favors."

"But you don't think that explains her behavior at the funeral?"

"No," Meade said. "Everything she said seemed calculated. It might've been literally true, but it felt like she was giving me what she thought I wanted to hear."

"In other words," Tower said, "you don't trust her."

"She definitely wants me to trust her. That part was obvious."

The dining room of the Douglass Café and Barbecue had been empty all morning, except for Tower, Meade, and Lucinda. Now it contained one more person. Margaret Douglass had slipped quietly through the kitchen door and taken a seat behind Lucinda and Meade. Tower saw her enter but gave no sign of acknowledgment.

"Lucinda, what's your assessment of our new friend Catherine Parrish?"

"She acts quiet and unassuming, but there's an intensity underneath that. A drive. She works hard to appear harmless, but I don't believe that's who she is. She's up to something, and she told me very little the other night."

Tower leaned back in his chair and glanced past Lucinda and

Meade. They turned and saw Margaret.

"Meade, I believe you know this young lady," Tower said. "Lucinda, I'd like you to meet Margaret Douglass."

Lucinda rose and crossed to Margaret, taking her hand warmly. "Margaret, I'm so pleased to meet you. Meade has spoken very highly of you."

"Margaret, would you join us at the table, please?" Tower invited.

As she sat down, Tower added, "Margaret and I have been working together. We've decided that she needs to be part of this operation."

Recovering from his surprise, Meade asked, "Were you working with Commander Tower when we talked the other day?"

"Yes, I was," she said simply.

"Margaret has many talents, Meade, as you well know," Tower said. "She's an excellent map reader and cartographer. And she's on her way to becoming a first-class cryptologist."

"Thank you, Commander," Lucinda said. "Now, let's talk about Catherine Parrish. I have something I think you should all see."

Lucinda reached into her purse and pulled out two pieces of paper, spreading them on the table. Margaret leaned forward, examining them both. She picked one up, then the other, holding them together.

"These were typed on the same typewriter," she said.

Lucinda nodded. "That's what I thought." Margaret passed the papers to Tower, who studied them closely.

"What are these?" he asked.

"The one in your left hand is the note left on our doorstep two nights ago," Lucinda explained. "It's why Meade rushed down to E Street."

"And the other?"

Lucinda looked at Meade. "You should tell him."

Meade took a breath. "That note came to me on the day the admiral was killed. It showed up on my desk at the *Washington Beacon*. At the time, it didn't seem too unusual—I didn't know much about the admiral's routines."

"So you followed its instructions?" Tower asked.

"I did, though I was a little late getting there."

"And when you arrived, you found the admiral dead. Was anyone else in the building?"

"Yes. Someone was hiding in the hallway outside the admiral's office. I didn't see who it was, but once I was inside, I heard footsteps. There was also the night watchman—he came into the office while I was still there."

"Did he see you?"

"No. I hid behind a small desk."

"But he raised the alarm?"

"Yes, and while he was doing that, I slipped out the back and made my way through the alleys. When I came back onto E Street, the police were arriving. I ducked into the Townhouse Saloon."

"And that's where you ran into Burley O'Malley?"

"Yes."

"And you've never told anyone about that night?"

Lucinda interjected. "Commander, Meade told me, and we decided it was best to keep it between us."

Tower sat stony-faced. His first instinct was anger—but he had learned to suppress personal reactions. What mattered was: *What does this new information mean? And how can I use it?*

"And now you have a second note, likely from the same source.

What do you make of that?"

Lucinda and Meade exchanged a look.

"I think someone is trying to manipulate Meade," Lucinda said.

"And you believe that someone is Catherine Parrish?"

"I think it's very likely. She showed up at exactly the right moment. A clever way to gain his trust."

Tower looked at them both, as though weighing possibilities.

"I think you're right," he said.

The silence that followed was heavy with understanding. Each person in the room grasped that something significant had just been confirmed. Especially Tower, who realized he was finally in a position to act decisively.

Faint sounds came from the kitchen—pans clattering, voices murmuring. Only Margaret seemed to know what they meant.

Tower turned toward her, about to speak, when the kitchen door opened. Dennis Douglass entered, carrying a heaping plate of food. Behind him was a small woman with a tray of dishes and utensils. They marched in like a parade.

"Whatever you folks are talking about," Dennis declared, "it's time to quit and eat some lunch."

Everyone laughed.

Meade stood to greet Dennis, introducing him to Lucinda. Dennis introduced his wife, Priscilla—the proud mother of Margaret. The next half hour was filled with eating, laughter, and light conversation.

Later, Lucinda asked to see the kitchen. Meade and Dennis discussed the restaurant and its connection to Frederick Douglass. Tower and Margaret whispered quietly in the corner.

When the meal ended, Dennis brought in a fresh pot of coffee.

Tower stood and called the group back together.

"Now," he said, "we need to hear from Margaret."

She sat up straight, shuffling a few papers. When she began, her voice was clear and deliberate.

"Sometime ago, Commander Tower asked me to gather information about an organization he wasn't sure even existed."

Tower interrupted: "Let me just say that Margaret is a remarkable young woman. Her talents go far beyond maps and codes. She has access to a network of people none of us do."

He paused. "Excuse me, Margaret. Please continue."

"Thank you. What the Commander calls a 'network' is just my family and friends. I never thought of it that way until he used the term."

She continued.

"The organization we're looking into may not be a true organization yet. I'll break it down into three elements: 'signals,' which are confirmed facts; 'signs,' which are things we suspect; and 'noise,' which is general talk or sentiment."

She explained that barroom chatter about the heroism of the Confederacy was *noise*. Violent anti-government statements might be a *sign*. Specific names or locations would be a *signal*.

"At present, we don't have any definitive signals. But we do have some signs—and quite a bit of noise."

Everyone leaned in.

"We believe a group may be forming—loose, informal, but real—of people opposed to the United States government. Many of them are children of Confederate soldiers. They've inherited bitterness, if not open hostility."

"Exactly who they are and what they intend, we don't yet know.

Commander Tower has made initial attempts to place a loyal agent among them."

She added: "We suspect Catherine Parrish may be at the center—but for now, that's just a sign."

Lucinda and Meade exchanged glances. They both sensed the gravity of what Margaret was describing.

"One final thing," she said. "As far as we can tell, this group doesn't yet have a name. So we've given it one: *The Second Generation.*"

Again, silence.

It was Tower who broke it. "The question now is—what's next?"

36: The Committee

Nathan Tower was slightly shorter than average for a man of his time, though not noticeably so. He was powerfully built, with easy, deliberate movements that tended to put people at ease. His face, framed by short sideburns, was unusually smooth for someone who had spent so many years at sea.

By all rights, Tower should have been a captain or admiral by now. He had graduated from Annapolis, and his wartime service was enviable. But unlike most naval officers, he was more interested in people than ships.

He loved observing, analyzing motives, and working behind the scenes to protect the country—even when no war had been declared.

Officially, Tower oversaw the assignment of naval attachés to embassies worldwide. He performed this role dutifully. But his true superiors—the ones who mattered—knew he was involved in something else, something they had been quietly told not to ask about.

Now, in the aftermath of the meeting at the Douglass Café and Barbecue, Tower looked at the three people in front of him: Meade, Lucinda, and Margaret. Burley O'Malley was missing—he was already on assignment and would be briefed later.

"You've all heard this in some form," Tower said, "but let me emphasize: this isn't a game. This is serious—and dangerous. Admiral Radford was murdered, and his killer tried to make it look like suicide. Whoever did it won't hesitate to kill again."

He looked each of them in the eye. Their faces told him they understood.

And with that, Tower had something he had long hoped for: a true espionage team.

"So, Commander Tower," Lucinda said, "what are our next steps?"

"I prefer 'Nathan,'" he said, smiling.

"Nathan," she repeated.

He looked at Margaret. "We need to turn Catherine Parrish from a sign into a signal. If she really is at the center, we need to prove it."

"I think we're close," Lucinda said.

"But we need confirmation," Margaret added.

"That's your task," Tower said. "Burley has confirmed she works in the Navy Yard's accounting department. First, find the typewriter she uses. See if it matches the notes you have."

"I can do that," Lucinda said. "It would be easier if she's not there."

"I'll have her assigned to my office for the day," Tower said. "She'll be gone by mid-morning."

"Does she have a personnel record?" Margaret asked.

"Yes, and I'll have it sent to my office tomorrow. You and Lucinda can review it and plan how to dig deeper into her background."

Margaret and Lucinda both nodded.

Tower turned to Meade. "Stay close to Catherine. Make her think you're getting close to finding the maps."

In other words, lead her on—while trying to figure out how much she's leading me on.

"Exactly."

Then Tower added, "Meade, I want you to do one more thing. Sit down with your father. Over lunch or dinner. Talk to him. Ask him about his life, his work—whatever comes to mind. I have a feeling something useful might come out of it."

Meade pulled out his notebook, half-smiling. "Lunch with my father—per Nathan's request."

Tower smiled too. "Let's regroup here in a week and see what we've learned."

As Tower moved to rise, Lucinda raised a hand.

"What about the money?"

Tower met her gaze. "I know you're not asking for payment. I know your family's position. You're asking how this operation is funded."

"That's right," she said. Her voice carried a tone that demanded an honest answer.

"Congress hasn't authorized this work," Tower said. "There's no official appropriation. A few Navy leaders support us—and funnel funds from other accounts."

"But it's not enough," Lucinda said. "Shall I mention *the committee*?"

Tower didn't flinch.

"That name," he said, "must stay in this room."

He let the silence linger before continuing.

"We have a group of private individuals—not members of Congress—who understand the need for espionage. They have resources. They've funded us—and pledged to continue."

"And our father is one of them," Meade said.

Tower paused, then replied, "For now, I won't go beyond what

I've already said."

37: Cumberland County

L AWD, HONEY, THEM PARRISHES—THEY was mean ones. This county been a lot better off since they gone."

"Are all of them gone?" Margaret asked. "Anyone left?"

"Far as I know, they all cleared out some years back—not that anybody noticed or even cared."

"That daddy of theirs, he was a big talker. Bad to drink, too. Liked to brag about how he fought for the Confederates, even when nobody in this county put much stock in that. Folks up here was pretty much for the Union."

"Yeah, he'd get hisself drunk and talk about all that, and the families that lost folks—they didn't like it. But it didn't stop him none. He just bragged and carried on like he was some kind of Bobby Lee."

"What about his children?" Margaret asked.

Etta White had to think. "Had five of 'em, far as I remember. Oldest one was a girl—her name was Kit or Cat, or some such. Then there was three boys, and a little girl at the end. Thing about that last little girl—she was a pretty little thing, prettier than her older sister."

"What do you remember about the older sister?"

"Mean as a snake. Always into something—sneakin' around, gettin' her brothers to do mean stuff."

Etta's son, Malcolm, chimed in: "They burned down one of

our barns, that one belonged to cousin Dale. You remember that, Mama?"

"Do I remember it? What you talkin' about, boy? That barn had a bunch of hay in it. Good thing we didn't have no horses in there."

"What happened with the barn?"

"Nothing happened at all. It just burned. We knew who did it—it was them Parrishes. We complained, but nobody paid attention. Wasn't too long after that, they was gone—and we was glad to see the back of 'em."

Margaret had been at the White family home, on a deserted country road outside Cumberland, for over an hour, listening to stories from Etta White—the grand dame of the family—and her kin. It was Friday morning, two days after the meeting at the Douglass Café and Barbecue. Margaret hadn't imagined then that she'd be in the mountains of Maryland, listening to family lore—some useful, some not.

Lester Douglass told me you was comin'. What's a pretty little thing like you doin' askin' about the Parrishes? Come all the way from Washington, did you?

Lester Douglass was one of the people Tower had identified as part of Margaret's "network." After the discoveries Margaret and Lucinda had made on Thursday, Margaret put out the word that she wanted to talk to someone in Cumberland County. It didn't take long to find the Whites.

"You gonna stay for lunch, honey?"

Margaret tried to politely decline, but the family wouldn't hear of it.

"Malcolm's wife, Betty, is in there cookin' up some fresh greens right now," Etta said proudly. "Little thing like you gotta start eatin' right. You ain't gonna have no bones on you when it comes time to give your husband some young-uns."

Oh Lord, Margaret groaned inwardly, *but I'd better not offend anyone.*

She smiled broadly and said, "I'd love to stay, Mrs. White. Thank you very much."

**

In another part of the county, Lucinda was hearing much the same story—but from a different source.

On Thursday morning, it hadn't taken long for Lucinda to confirm that the notes she'd received had come from Catherine Parrish's typewriter. That afternoon, she and Margaret had visited Commander Tower's office to examine Catherine's personnel file. Her hometown was listed as Cumberland, Maryland.

By that evening, Lucinda and Margaret were on a train bound for Cumberland. Lucinda booked two first-class seats, fully expecting trouble. As soon as the conductor came around for tickets, he stopped at their row. Seeing Margaret in first class, he took on a pompous air and began telling her she needed to move to the third-class coach.

But before he got three words out, Lucinda interrupted him, raising her voice slightly.

"Excuse me, sir, she is traveling with me."

The conductor wasn't used to being challenged—especially not by a woman.

"And who might you be, madam?"

Lucinda looked him in the eye. "My name is Mrs. Robert Siegel." She paused for effect. "Does that name mean anything to you?"

Then she sat down again, pretending to read her book.

Robert Siegel was the vice president of the railroad line they were riding. Lucinda had never met him but knew enough to bluff convincingly if she had to.

The conductor stared at her a moment, then moved on without another word.

When the train arrived in Cumberland near midnight, Lucinda had already arranged for them to stay at the Cumberland Mountain Hotel, just steps from the station. The sleepy night clerk checked them in without incident. The next morning, they ordered breakfast in their room, reviewed their plan, and set out separately. One of Margaret's cousins picked her up with a wagon, and she was at the White family home in no time.

Lucinda's investigation was even easier.

On Thursday evening, she had contacted a senator from Maryland, who connected her with a friend in Cumberland County. That friend recommended a retired schoolteacher named Melvin O'Brien. If anyone knew the Parrish family, it was him. Conveniently, he lived only a few blocks from Lucinda's hotel.

About the time Margaret was sitting with the White family, Lucinda entered O'Brien's modest home. Books lined the walls of the tidy parlor where he offered her tea.

"Why are you askin' about the Parrishes?" O'Brien asked, once Lucinda was settled.

"This is simply a routine check for an important government position," she said vaguely. "I'm afraid I can't say more than that right now."

O'Brien accepted the explanation easily. He was nearly seventy and styled himself a gentleman of the old school—courteous, well-spoken, and fond of the company of a pretty woman. He explained that his wife had died years ago but that he kept the house just as she would've liked.

"The Parrishes were certainly an interesting family," he said once they had tea. "Five kids. I had them all in my class at one time. The youngest was only four or five, but their mother had passed, and there was nowhere else for her to go."

"What about the father?"

"James Parrish was an odd one. Most people around here were Union folks, and a lot had sons who'd enlisted. Parrish made a point of announcing that he'd fought for the Rebs. That didn't go over well. People around here didn't like it, especially those who'd lost kin in the war. He was shunned."

"Shunned?"

"Well, nobody paid him much mind. He was drunk most of the time, and folks figured he wasn't worth arguing with."

Lucinda sipped her tea. "What kind of effect did that have on the children?"

O'Brien nodded gravely. "It was hard. They kept to themselves. Didn't have any friends. If anything bad happened, folks blamed them. Probably not always fair—but they didn't make it easy, either."

He paused. "Bright kids, though. All of them. Especially the oldest girl—Kitty, I think they called her. Sharp as a tack. Never worked hard, but didn't have to. They were quick."

"What happened to their father?"

"Fell over dead one day. Heart attack, they said—though drink probably had something to do with it."

He added that the father's death had a powerful effect on the children. "They idolized him. Followed him everywhere. He told them stories—Confederate stuff, mostly. They worshiped him."

"And after he died?"

"That was around '72 or '73. They stopped coming to school. I remember asking the sheriff to check on them, but nothing came of it."

"Do you remember their names?"

He thought. "No, not all. The youngest was called Jumper, but that was a nickname. The oldest was Kathy—Catherine, maybe?"

Lucinda was about to leave when O'Brien's eyes lit up.

"Say, I think I've got something."

He left the room. While he was gone, Lucinda walked quietly around the living room. She studied a framed photograph of O'Brien and his wife in their younger days and wondered if they'd ever had children. There was no sign of any.

O'Brien returned with a photograph.

"I used to dabble in photography. Took pictures of my students. This one here—that's the Parrish kids. Last year they were in school."

He handed it to her. The children were lined up from oldest to youngest. Catherine looked about fourteen, standing beside a tall boy—perhaps John.

"And you don't remember the youngest girl's name?"

He looked again at the photo. "The boys were John, James, and Charles. But no, I just can't remember the little one's name."

38: Hubert Meadows

"**Y**OU NEVER TOLD US you were a spy."

Meade Meadows sat across from his father in the dining room of the Imperial Hotel. It was Friday at lunch. That wasn't how Meade had planned to begin the conversation, but since Commander Tower's revelation, the thought had weighed on him.

Hubert wasn't surprised. "It wasn't something I could share with you children at the time. After the war, it didn't seem important anymore."

"Nathan Tower says you helped the Union take Fort Donelson."

"Nathan's probably right about that."

"That sounds pretty significant to me," Meade said. "I'd be crowing about it if I'd done it."

"A good spy doesn't crow," Hubert noted.

Their meals had arrived, and both began eating.

"I assume Nathan told you why we're talking today."

"He did. And I'm glad he made the suggestion. We haven't always found it easy to talk, have we?"

"No," Meade admitted. "And if I'm being honest, some of that's been my fault."

"You've always had strong opinions," Hubert said with a chuckle. "But don't shoulder all the blame. I played my part."

They shared a quiet moment as a waiter refilled their water glasses. For the next few minutes, they touched on family, business, and Meade's work at the *Washington Beacon*.

Then a memory surfaced.

"Papa," Meade said, "do you remember a man named Luther? He worked in your carpentry shop."

Hubert's face lit up. "Luther Jones. Best carpenter I ever had. He liked you, too—liked showing you things in the shop."

"I thought of him the other day. How did you hire him?"

"He was a Union soldier, stationed in Nashville. After the Battle of Nashville, I learned he'd been badly wounded. I brought him home, had him mustered out, and once he recovered, he started working for me."

"He made beautiful furniture," Meade recalled.

"Yes, he did. And he was a good manager. After the war, we had big orders—tables, desks, chairs. A lot of that furniture ended up here in Washington."

Hubert smiled with pride. "Some of it's still in use today."

That afternoon, Meade sat at his desk at the *Beacon*, still reflecting on the conversation with his father. In a quiet moment, the name *Luther Jones* flashed across his mind. He saw the workshop, the carpentry tools, the furniture...

Wait.

Meade sat bolt upright.

I know where the maps are.

At the center of the newsroom sat three telephones. Meade picked up one and called Commander Tower's office. A clerk answered.

"Commander Tower is out for the afternoon."

"Do you know where he is?"

"No, sir."

Meade hung up. But he had a very good idea where the Commander was.

He stepped out onto Pennsylvania Avenue, hailed a carriage, and climbed in.

"Take me to Seventh Street Athletic Park," he said.

39: The Diplomat

"THE MAPS ARE IN our possession."

The voice of the American cut through the darkness of Oak Hill Cemetery, startling the Diplomat.

He had been standing in the cold and damp of that April night—close to midnight—waiting for the American. The message summoning him had said the matter was urgent. Usually, when the American requested a meeting, it was at the most inconvenient time. Tonight was no different. He had been attending an embassy party, and his chances of seducing one of the beautiful guests had been excellent.

Instead, he was here in this godforsaken cemetery, alone in the dark, the cold seeping through his light jacket. He had stumbled his way to the designated spot, guided only by the precise instructions the American had given. At their last meeting, he had been the one in charge—but that time had passed. She now controlled the operation. He had no choice but to follow her lead.

This is beneath me. A diplomat, skulking around like a thief. And for what?

These resentments had built steadily as he waited longer than he thought reasonable.

Then suddenly, her voice.

He turned toward the sound. He heard the faint rustle of movement, but still saw nothing.

The news she brought, however, dissolved much of his irritation. It was the news he had been waiting to hear.

"You have the maps. Where are they?" he asked.

Again, a slight sound—maybe a step, maybe a shift—but no figure emerged.

The voice was odd. A little strange, perhaps, but it was saying something he wanted—*needed*—to hear.

"Not so fast," she said. **"You'll get your maps in good time and in good order, but certain things must happen first."**

"You're demanding more money?" he said, his voice low and edged with anger.

"More money would certainly be welcomed," she replied. **"A nice bonus for a job well done. You might want to consider that. But no—money isn't why we're here."**

"This is about getting away then," he said. **"I can have you out of Washington and aboard one of our ships by noon tomorrow."**

"It is about getting away," she said, **"but we have to do it our way—not yours."**

"Why? What do you mean?"

"We're being watched. I'm sure of it. If we tried to run now, we'd be caught."

The Diplomat was silent for a moment, processing.

Of course you're being watched. You've bungled nearly everything so far.

"You have a plan, I suppose," he said, sarcasm creeping into his voice despite his effort to suppress it.

"Yes, of course I have a plan. But you must be ready to act, and follow every instruction we give you—exactly and without delay."

"And when do we get the maps?"

"You'll get the maps as soon as we are safely out of Washington."

"Then what do you need from me?"

"We'll need a small, enclosed carriage with one driver. You will need to be inside the carriage."

She laid out the plan for the escape. It was simple, and it didn't take long for her to explain.

"You must follow these instructions exactly. Be ready to move when we give the signal."

"I understand," the Diplomat said.

Then, a final rustle—and she was gone.

Finally. An end to this wretched operation. An end to the American woman I've come to despise.

If this succeeded, his government would finally receive the maps they were so desperate to obtain.

And he would receive the glory.

40: The Plan

Commander Nathan Tower sat in the dining room of the Douglass Café and Barbecue on T Street, struggling to shake a feeling of amazement. He was listening to his team deliver their individual reports, and though he had expected solid work, he had not anticipated results this fast.

What surprised him wasn't just the quality of their findings—it was how quickly everything had come together. He had expected the operation to stretch out over several weeks. Instead, they had reached this point in just three days.

The photograph Lucinda had brought back from Cumberland County lay on the table in front of him. For the fourth—no, fifth—time, he picked it up and examined it closely, looking at each face, starting with the eldest: Catherine.

She was now a *signal*, as Margaret Douglass had termed it—not just a vague suspicion, but a clear and focused presence in the fog of espionage.

Margaret was speaking again, recounting how she had found the White family through some of her cousins. The Whites had been welcoming, treating her like a long-lost friend rather than the stranger she was.

As she spoke, Tower kept looking at the photograph. The

youngest child at the end of the row—the little girl—struck him. Something about her seemed familiar. Lucinda had said she couldn't have been more than four or five years old. She was quite beautiful—noticeably more so than her older sister. Perhaps that's what drew his eye. But Tower couldn't shake the feeling there was something more.

Where have I seen that face?

Margaret, grinning, confessed she hadn't much enjoyed the home-cooked greens served for lunch—but the buttermilk pie more than made up for it.

Everyone laughed.

Lucinda and Meade each asked Margaret clarifying questions.

Then Tower turned to Meade. "Now, let's hear from the star of the show."

Meade had clearly been waiting for this moment. He and Lucinda had ridden together in a carriage to the café, and though she knew he was sitting on something important, he hadn't told her. Tower had specifically instructed him not to.

Meade began by reminiscing about the carpentry shop in his father's business and how much he'd loved watching the work as a child.

Tower interrupted with a grin. "Meade, give us the headline first."

"I've figured out where the maps are," Meade said.

Lucinda and Margaret both let out audible reactions of approval.

"How?" Lucinda asked.

Meade explained: he had watched the master carpenter at his father's shop—a man named Luther—build a particular kind of desk. *I may have actually seen him building that desk,* he said.

The desk in Admiral Radford's study, he realized, was the same model. "It had a secret compartment," he explained. "That's where the maps are. I'm sure of it."

Lucinda raised an eyebrow. "You haven't checked to make sure?"

Meade started to answer, but Tower spoke first. "No—we haven't checked. And we won't. The maps need to stay right where they are, for now."

He moved quickly into the plan.

Tower wanted Meade to arrange a meeting with Catherine Parrish that very afternoon. At that meeting, Meade would tell her that he had figured out where the maps were—specifically, that they were hidden in the admiral's desk.

Then, Meade would say that he had unavoidable obligations early that evening, but planned to retrieve the maps later that night. He would invite her to come along—after all, she had shown such interest in the admiral and had been helpful.

"We have people watching Catherine now," Tower said. "Burley's in charge of that. He'll have lookouts posted near the admiral's office by the time Meade meets with her."

Tower's expectation was that Catherine would try to retrieve the maps immediately after learning their location. "By the time we get there," he said, "the maps will be gone—and so will she."

Lucinda interjected, "But your plan is to have someone already there when she tries to steal them."

"That's correct," Tower said. "And not just someone—I want *us* to be there."

He explained: Catherine had to be caught in the act. He wanted her to find the maps and take them out, so there would be no question as to her guilt.

"When she arrives," he said, "Meade and I will already be inside the admiral's office—hidden. Even if she turns on the lights, she won't see us."

He looked at Lucinda and Margaret.

"I'd like the two of you in the office across the hall. I don't know whether Catherine will be armed, but it's very possible. If she pulls a gun or tries to run, you'll be there. If not, we'll call you in."

Everyone in the room nodded.

The plan was set.

Each person knew their role, their location, and the timing.

Now it was just a matter of execution.

41: The Alleyway

A SMALL, ENCLOSED CARRIAGE pulled by two horses passed within a few feet of the watchful eyes of Burley O'Malley. Burley stood in the shadows of the April evening at the corner of the alleyway that ran behind E Street and the building where the admiral's office was located. From his vantage point, he could see all the way down to E Street in one direction and to the next street over in the other.

It was well after six o'clock, and darkness had overtaken most of Washington, D.C. Street lamps provided light on main thoroughfares like E Street, but the alleyways remained unlit. Burley could see little beyond vague shapes and outlines.

As expected, the carriage came to a stop behind the building. Burley stepped out of the shadows slightly, moving just far enough to get a clear view of the space between the carriage and the rear door.

The carriage, driver, and horses stood perfectly still. They remained that way for what felt to Burley like an unusually long time—only one or two minutes in reality, but long enough to raise questions in his mind.

Is something wrong?

Have I been seen?

Has the carefully constructed plan Commander Tower devised somehow been exposed?

With each second that passed, his anxiety grew. His orders were simple: stay where he was and observe. He quietly repeated the instruction to himself like a calming mantra, resisting the urge to act.

Stay put. Watch. Wait. Don't jump the gun.

Then, suddenly, everything was as it should be.

A figure emerged from the carriage. Dressed in a long coat with a cape and a hood, the figure was short—just as he expected. Without hesitation, she stepped onto the ground and moved directly toward the rear entrance. She didn't pause. She didn't glance in either direction down the alley. She went straight into the building.

Burley turned and looked toward E Street. There, in the middle of the alley, stood one of Tower's operatives. Burley signaled to him using a prearranged gesture. The operative responded with an acknowledgment and relayed the signal to someone positioned near the front of the building—letting those inside know that Catherine Parrish had entered.

Burley turned his attention back to the alley—only to see something he had not expected.

The carriage driver straightened, picked up the reins, and urged the horses forward. The carriage rumbled slowly down the alley. At the far end, it turned left and disappeared.

Burley frowned.

What the hell?

It's supposed to stay put.

Tower never said what to do if it left.

In fact, Tower had specifically told him that at some point in the evening, he was to approach the carriage and apprehend anyone inside—or nearby. But now, the carriage was gone.

Maybe it's just circling the block to avoid suspicion, he reasoned.

Burley briefly considered chasing it—but knew he couldn't abandon his post. Someone might still exit through the rear. He felt confident the carriage would return soon.

So he stayed put and waited.

42: Inside the Building

T HE PETITE FIGURE STEPPED through the back door of the building and ascended the rear staircase, emerging onto the third floor where Admiral Radford's office was located. She wore a floor-length dress beneath a dark cloak with a hood that concealed her head and most of her face. Despite the length of her skirts, she climbed the stairs easily, lifting the fabric just enough to keep it from tangling around her shoes. In her left hand, she carried a small lantern, unlit.

At the top of the stairs, she paused—still and silent.

She listened.

Faint sounds drifted in from *E Street*, muffled and distant. It was Saturday night, and the usual revelry of that district was beginning to reach full volume. A small window at the end of the hallway let in a dim glow, but not enough to see clearly.

She waited, holding her breath, listening for any noise from inside the building.

Nothing.

Satisfied, she started down the hallway toward the admiral's office. Every few steps, she paused and listened again. Her eyes were adjusting to the low light, and she could begin to make out the doors and nameplates along the corridor.

At last, she reached the office door. It was closed. She gripped the handle and turned it slowly, hoping it wouldn't squeak. It clicked softly—but not loud enough to be heard beyond her own ears.

She eased the door open. It creaked faintly.

She froze, listening.

Still nothing.

Gaining confidence, she stepped inside.

The windows at the front of the office allowed in a soft glow from the streetlamps outside. She could see well enough to identify objects within the room—most notably, the admiral's desk, the reason she had come.

She paused for a moment, then took a match from her pocket and struck it against the lantern. The flame flared, and she slipped it inside. The lantern lit with a warm glow. She blew out the match and set it aside.

The light was enough to illuminate the desk and her next move.

She opened the top drawer and found a small key. She pulled the drawer completely free of the desk and placed it gently on the floor.

Then she knelt down and crawled underneath.

Just as Meade had done at the admiral's home, she found the hidden lock—the one obscured by the top drawer. She inserted the key.

A moment later, she backed out from beneath the desk. She placed the lantern on top of it.

And then the lights came on.

Electric light flooded the room. Two men stood before her.

"Catherine Parrish," one of them said, "you're under arrest."

The cloaked woman didn't flinch. She didn't seem surprised—neither by the light nor the sudden appearance of Commander Nathan Tower and Meade Meadows.

Her hands were empty. Calmly, she reached up and pushed back the hood, letting it fall behind her shoulders.

"Commander Tower," she said. "Mr. Meadows. Good evening. As you can see—"

She smiled faintly.

"—*I am not Catherine Parrish.*"

Tower and Meade stared.

The woman before them was Julia—the maid who had poured their tea at Mary Mae Radford's house.

"*My name is Julia,*" she said. "*Julia Parrish.*"

43: The Small Carriage

THE SMALL CARRIAGE THAT Burley O'Malley had seen disappear after it deposited the petite figure in the alleyway came to a stop after several turns. Though it had only traveled a few blocks from *E Street*, its route had been deliberately circuitous.

Inside were two passengers. One was Catherine Parrish, wearing the same black cloak as her sister, though the hood was down, revealing her face. The other was the Diplomat—Diego Ferdinand Martinez. A rather large man, Martinez looked uncomfortable in the cramped interior. He was accustomed to traveling in greater luxury.

Still, he had done exactly as instructed. A few days earlier, he had secured this modest carriage, and now, at Catherine Parrish's signal, he had put their escape plan into motion. His discomfort gave way to satisfaction: *I have fulfilled the assignment my superiors gave me.*

"Your plan was a clever one," Martinez said. "Substituting your sister to evade surveillance—brilliant."

Catherine merely shrugged. *Compliments from this man mean nothing.*

"And now," he said, "may I have the maps?"

Catherine reached inside her cloak and drew out a bundle of navigational maps, rolled up and tied with string. She handed them to him.

"Don't we get some kind of bonus?" she said. "I think you mentioned that last time we spoke."

Martinez took the maps eagerly. Almost as an afterthought, he reached into his coat and handed her an envelope. It wasn't overflowing with cash, but the sum was significant.

Catherine counted the money quickly as Martinez unfolded the maps. There were at least a dozen, and together they formed a detailed rendering of Spain's coastline. He didn't examine them closely—he only needed to confirm they appeared authentic.

Looking up at Catherine, he said, "Now we need to get you onto the ship waiting in Baltimore Harbor. What about your sister?"

In the distance, they heard the clear clang of a ship's bell.

"My sister is not your concern," Catherine replied. "Let's get going."

She tapped the roof of the carriage. The driver snapped the reins, and the horses broke into motion. The carriage turned east and was soon swallowed by the darkness.

44: Julia Parrish

JULIA PARRISH SPREAD HER arms wide so Nathan Tower could see both palms. Her hands were empty.

"Commander, please lower your gun," she said. The calm confidence in her voice was striking. "As you can see, I am not armed. I realize I'm under arrest, as you say—but I expect to be free before long."

Tower lowered the pistol.

"Thank you," she said. "Now, I need to do two things."

Julia stood behind the admiral's desk. Tower and Meade remained in the corners where they had been hidden. Without warning, Julia turned and took a step toward the ship's bell that the admiral had proudly displayed while alive. She grabbed the clapper and let it strike the bell once.

The sound rang out—clear and loud—echoing for blocks.

"What is she doing?" Meade asked.

"Giving her sister a signal," Tower said with a faint smile. "She's just told her that everything is fine—and that she can disappear."

"Excellent, Commander," Julia said, impressed. "Very perceptive."

"If her sister is this close," Meade said, "can't we go after her? Try to catch her?"

Tower shook his head. "She's at least several blocks away by now. We wouldn't know where to start. By the time we tried, she'd be long gone."

Julia returned to the desk.

"I'd like to point out," she said, addressing both men, "that the secret compartment inside this desk is empty. I do not have the maps. They're gone."

"Along with your sister," Tower said.

"That's correct."

Meade rushed to the desk and ducked beneath it. The secret compartment was indeed empty.

"What? How—?" he stammered. "I don't understand. How did Catherine get the maps?"

Julia crossed to the admiral's chair and sat down, perfectly composed. "If you gentlemen will take a seat, I can explain a few things."

Tower pulled up a chair and gestured for Meade to do the same. At that moment, Lucinda and Margaret—who had been hiding in the office across the hall—entered the room. Their surprise was evident when they saw Julia instead of Catherine.

"This is Julia Parrish," Tower said by way of introduction. "Catherine's younger sister. She's offered to enlighten us."

Lucinda and Margaret exchanged looks of disbelief, then took the chairs Meade and Tower had just moved.

"As I said, Commander," Julia began, "I understand I'm under arrest. But you have no evidence tying me to the stolen maps. At most, I could be charged with breaking and entering. But I suspect, on reflection, you'll think better of that. I doubt you want a public trial where information about the maps becomes widely known."

She paused, gauging their reactions.

No response?

"Very well. Let me add this: under no circumstances will I reveal where my sister is or what she has done with those maps. Even if you prosecute me and lock me away, I will never speak of that."

Tower studied her face. "On that score," he said, "I believe you."

"There are other things I can tell you," she continued, "and still others I choose not to. Ask your questions. I'll answer what I can."

Tower focused on operational matters, but Julia's answers were vague—evasions more than revelations. It was clear, however, that Meade had a different question weighing on him.

"How did you get the maps out of the desk?" he asked. "We've been watching the office. Since I told Catherine how to access the compartment, no one has been near it."

Julia nodded, acknowledging his frustration. "That was my mistake. I should have realized it the night I came to your house, but I didn't. *If I'd figured it out sooner—before Catherine made contact with you—we wouldn't be sitting here right now.*"

She paused, then added, "Once I did realize it, a few days ago, the office wasn't being watched. It was easy enough for someone—not necessarily me—to break in and retrieve the maps. By that time, Catherine was under surveillance, so we had to devise a plan to free her from Washington and evade the Commander's prying eyes."

As she finished her answer, Lucinda reached into her purse and pulled out a photograph—the one she had obtained from the retired schoolmaster in Cumberland County. She leaned forward and handed it to Julia.

"Have you ever seen this before?"

Julia studied it intently. Her eyes filled with tears. "No. I never have."

Lucinda's voice softened. "What happened to you children after your father died?"

Julia cleared her throat and began to tell her story.

45: The Small Carriage

THE DIPLOMAT HAD TRIED several times during the first hour of the journey to begin a conversation with Catherine Parrish.

He began by describing his hometown in Spain and reminiscing about his childhood. Catherine expressed no interest. The more he talked, the less she responded.

A man used to success with women, he began to feel uneasy in her presence. He was seated very close to her in the cramped carriage. She wasn't what he considered beautiful, though she had attractive features. Still, he believed that any woman—*any* woman—could be wooed.

Next, he tried speaking about his role at the embassy: the daily routines, the ceremonies, the social circles, and finally, the more covert operations—the espionage assignments to which he had recently been entrusted.

Again, Catherine gave him little more than a few clipped responses. Eventually, even those stopped. The silence between them thickened. *The man is a fool,* she thought. *An utter fool.*

In his third attempt, he tried flattery. He complimented her on the cleverness of her operation, on how smoothly she had executed the plan, and how grateful his government would be for the documents she had secured.

To this, she offered a simple, neutral, "Thank you." What he really wanted was information—details about how her operation worked, who her companions were, and, especially, who the beautiful young woman was that he'd briefly encountered earlier that evening.

When he asked about the sister, Catherine fell completely silent. Her expression hardened. Her posture shifted. Whatever conversation they might have had was over.

Finally, he gave up. *If she wants to talk, she will.* He settled into the silence, frustrated. The journey would take hours. He had tried to pass the time, but it was clear no rapport would be formed.

The carriage rambled on in the darkness. The only sounds were the steady clop of hooves and the occasional squeak of the wheels and axles. Eventually, the Diplomat began to drift off—not fully asleep, but lulled by the gentle rocking of the carriage and the rhythmic noise of the road. As he started to doze, he glanced over and noticed Catherine. Her eyes were wide open.

A few minutes later, another sound broke through the stillness—the sharp clatter of horses' hooves. At first distant, it quickly grew louder, unmistakably approaching.

Then, without warning, the carriage driver shouted, "Whoa!" The horses halted.

The Diplomat straightened in his seat, alert again. He turned to Catherine—and froze. She had drawn a small pistol and was pointing it directly at his stomach.

"Get out," she said.

He opened his mouth to protest, but she raised the pistol, aiming now between his eyes.

"Do as I tell you. Right now."

There was nothing soft or uncertain in her voice. It was a command—and it left no room for argument.

The Diplomat pushed open the carriage door and stepped down onto the dirt road. The driver was already on the ground, standing silently to his right.

A wave of panic surged through the Diplomat. *I should run. I have to do something—anything.*

To his left, two mounted riders emerged from the dark, their horses barely visible. The men wore long black capes and wide-brimmed hats that shadowed their faces. One of them held a lantern, casting a dim, flickering light over the scene.

It was the last thing the Diplomat ever saw.

The knife that slit his throat was so sharp, he barely felt it. For a few seconds, he staggered, gasping. But he was dead before he hit the ground.

Catherine Parrish stepped out of the carriage. The pistol was gone. In her hands now was a bundle of rolled maps tied with string.

Behind the mounted men were two riderless horses. Without a word, Catherine and the driver mounted and rode off into the night, retracing the path from which the riders had come.

Moments later, the road fell into silence.

The carriage and the Diplomat's body were swallowed by darkness.

46: The Parrishes

Lucinda Meadows asked Julia, "What happened to your family when your father died?"

Julia took a deep breath. "Our mother had died soon after I was born, so that left us as orphans—except, not exactly."

"What do you mean by that?" Meade Meadows asked.

"You have to understand, I was only about five years old at the time, and I don't remember much of it clearly. I do have some memories of my father, but not of what happened immediately after he died. This is the story I've been told."

Julia explained that their father, knowing he was dying and that the children would be left alone, gave Catherine, then fifteen, specific instructions. She was to break into the Cumberland County courthouse late at night and alter the birth records—hers and her older brother's—so that Catherine would appear to be seventeen, and John, nearly fourteen, would appear to be sixteen.

"Catherine, as you probably know, is very clever," Julia said. "She and John had no trouble breaking into the courthouse and finding the records. They were able to alter Catherine's birth certificate, and for some reason, they created a new one for John. Apparently, that didn't present much difficulty."

By aging themselves on paper, they would avoid being taken by authorities or placed in an orphanage.

"And the two younger brothers?" Lucinda asked.

"Yes, James and Charles—we called them Jimmy and Chuck," Julia said.

"What happened to them?"

"They were sent to an orphanage in Baltimore," Julia replied. "Our father was too sick to come up with a plan for them. The only thing he told Catherine was, *'You'll think of something.'*"

"And did she?" Lucinda asked.

"Yes, actually. What I'm about to say sounds fantastic, and I'm not sure I believe all of it myself—but this is what I've been told."

Julia said Catherine and John went to Baltimore, found jobs, and lived near the orphanage to keep an eye on their brothers. Catherine worked part-time in a music hall, where she befriended someone skilled in theatrical makeup and disguise. With this person's help, she made herself look like a woman in her twenties. She did the same for John.

"They went to the orphanage posing as a married couple," Julia said. "They made up a story about having lost children at birth and wanting to adopt two little boys—preferably brothers, and preferably recently admitted. Jimmy and Chuck fit the bill perfectly."

"That's hard to believe," Meade said.

"Yes, it is," Julia agreed. "Which is why I'm skeptical. But Catherine and John love telling the story, and I suspect at least part of it is true. Either way, they got the boys out, and the four of them lived together in Baltimore."

"And what happened to you?" Lucinda asked.

"My story is different," Julia said. "After our father's funeral, a woman named Amelia Birdsong was visiting a cousin in Cumberland. She was a wealthy widow from Richmond, and she saw me coming out of the church. She asked her cousin who I was and what would happen to me."

The cousin explained the children were likely to be sent to an orphanage.

'Then I'll adopt that little girl,' Mrs. Birdsong reportedly said. And she did.

"She took me back to Richmond. I think she may have promised I'd see my siblings again, but I don't remember."

"She raised you?" Meade asked.

"Yes," Julia said. "I lived very comfortably. She was prominent in Richmond's social scene—especially among the Confederate elite. Hardly a day passed without some talk of the war, of government oppression in Washington, and of course, the phrase *'damn Yankees'* was as common as *'pass the salt.'*"

She received a good education, was taught to play piano, and embraced the customs of Southern high society.

"Did you know where your siblings were?" Lucinda asked.

"Not for a long time," Julia said. "When I was fourteen, I was sent to the Augusta Female Seminary in Staunton. It's where Richmond's best and brightest girls were educated, and I enjoyed it. I was more studious than most, but I still had a good time."

Tower spoke. "But you remembered your siblings?"

Julia nodded. "I always thought, *if I had the chance, I'd try to find them.* That chance came when I made a friend from Cumberland. She invited me to travel with her during a school break. While there, I found out something about what had happened to Catherine and the boys."

Julia said she secretly wrote to the orphanage in Baltimore. The director replied, saying the boys had been adopted by a kind Baltimore couple.

"It didn't take me long to track them down."

When she was nearly eighteen, Mrs. Birdsong died suddenly of typhoid fever.

"And you inherited everything," Tower said.

"Yes. I was her legal child and sole heir."

"That gave you the freedom—and means—to find your siblings," Tower said.

"It wasn't hard at all."

"And growing up," Tower continued, "you were surrounded by the idea that the South had once been glorious. That the slaves were happy. That the Yankees were monsters. That honor and chivalry guided the South, while the North was cruel and corrupt."

"I heard all of that," Julia admitted.

Margaret, who had remained silent, finally spoke. "And have you heard of something called *The Second Generation*?"

Julia looked directly at her, then at Tower. "I think I've finished answering questions. I trust you won't detain me much longer."

Everyone stirred, except Julia, who continued to stare at Tower. He held her gaze, clearly weighing options.

"If you're thinking you can let me go and I'll lead you to Catherine, you're mistaken," Julia said. "I don't know where she is, and I don't expect to hear from her for a while."

With that, she stood and walked out of the admiral's office.

No one tried to stop her.

47: The Douglass Café and Barbecue

I N THE THREE DAYS following the events in the admiral's office that Saturday night, the biggest story in Washington was the mysterious death of a high-level Spanish diplomat. His body had been found on a country road somewhere between the city and Baltimore.

The scene raised more questions than it answered: Why was he there? The diplomat was discovered near a small carriage still hitched to two horses. There was no sign of a driver. Tracks indicated other horses had been nearby, but the markings were confusing and inconclusive.

Why was he murdered?

The Washington Beacon, among others, described him as a confident man—but also a notorious ladies' man. Some papers hinted that he may have been killed by a jealous lover or husband. But those were just rumors. The only confirmed fact was that he was dead and alone.

The Spanish ambassador responded carefully. He met with State Department officials and issued polite but pointed statements about the safety of diplomatic postings. A Catholic mass was held in Spanish. And then, the incident was allowed to fade into Washington's churning gossip and politics.

Meanwhile, Meade Meadows had expected to be assigned to the story. But Nathan Tower had contacted *Beacon* editor George Hudson and specifically asked that Meade not be assigned. Meade was surprised—but suspected the murder might be connected to Admiral Radford's death.

The case's outcome left him deeply unsettled. He had expected Catherine Parrish to be captured and charged with espionage—or worse. But she had escaped.

Now, Meade sat in the Douglass Café and Barbecue with the others from that night, the bitter taste of failure still in his mouth. It was strong enough that he broke his silence and asked—perhaps a little too sharply—"Why didn't you prosecute Julia, at least for breaking and entering?"

Tower wasn't offended. He looked at Meade, then the others.

"You can rarely rely on the legal system to bring justice," Tower said. "Those of us in espionage live in a legal no-man's-land."

Lucinda spoke. "Like Meade—and probably the rest of us—I'm frustrated by what happened. But I understand Nathan's point. Most of the case against Julia would involve things we'd never want to come out in public." She turned to Meade. "I hope you can understand that."

Meade nodded slightly, and the room fell into silence—tense and unsatisfying.

Then Tower stood. "I have a piece of news that might lift our spirits."

He looked toward the kitchen and raised his voice. "Professor Watkins, will you join us, please?"

Sylvester Watkins entered, carrying a large satchel. Behind him came Hubert Meadows, and then Burley O'Malley.

"I know many of you have felt defeated by the Parrishes and their so-called Second Generation," Tower said, "but that's not the case, as you're about to see."

He gestured to Watkins.

Watkins placed the satchel on the table, untied the string, and rolled out several sheets. The one on top was a detailed navigational map of the Spanish coast.

The group leaned in, eyes wide, voices buzzing with questions.

"These," Tower said, "are the real maps. The authentic charts created by Professor Watkins and his team—including Margaret Douglass. They're the most accurate surveys of the Spanish coastline available anywhere."

Tower paused. "I'm pleased to tell you that the maps the Parrishes stole were fakes. Specially designed decoys—laden with inaccuracies and false information."

"In other words," Meade said, "you wanted them to steal them."

"Yes," Tower confirmed.

Questions erupted: "How?" "Why?" "When?"

Tower raised his hand.

"I'll explain everything in detail, but here's the overview: from the start, I suspected that word of this project would leak. And that someone—some group—would try to steal the maps. Our objective wasn't only to protect the real maps, but to find out who was behind the espionage. And we did."

Margaret spoke up. "By exposing the Parrishes—and the Second Generation."

"Exactly," Tower said. "We now know who they are and how they operate."

"What else do we know?" Lucinda asked.

"We know the Parrishes are brilliant, organized, and deeply loyal to one another. But we also know they are ruthless. If murder is required, they won't hesitate."

"Like the admiral," Tower said.

"And the Spanish diplomat," Margaret added.

"Correct," Tower replied.

Lucinda leaned forward. "Those are things we know. But what do you think?"

Tower nodded. "I believe this Second Generation group, though rooted in old Confederate ideals, has evolved. They know the Confederacy isn't coming back. They've turned to something else."

He glanced at Margaret. "I checked with the Augusta Seminary. Julia Parrish took a strong interest in global politics and European diplomacy. My guess is this group now sees itself as an intelligence operation—stealing information and selling it to the highest bidder."

Tower looked at the group. "The diplomat found dead on Sunday had nothing on him. No maps. No papers. I believe the Parrishes promised him the maps—and then killed him. They kept the fakes. Now, they'll try to sell them elsewhere."

"And when they do," Meade said, "they'll be exposed as frauds."

"That's the plan," Tower said.

48: Nathan Tower

NATHAN TOWER SAT ALONE in an upstairs room of the house on Fourth Street. A half-filled glass of beer sat before him. Outside, darkness had once again overtaken Washington, D. C.—and that same darkness seemed to be overtaking his mind.

He had battled the Parrishes, who were working—at least in part—at the behest of the Spanish government. Tower asked himself: *Had I won? Or had I lost?* On balance, he could just about justify feeling that he'd come out ahead. *Maybe I'd scored more runs than my opponent.*

But, like in baseball, a team might lose today and return to play again tomorrow. In espionage, no opponent was ever fully defeated. They always came back for another game.

It was the game that mattered—stay ahead of your opponent, accept your losses, but keep playing.

Still, the thoughts were dark. Just as the April skies had turned gray again, Tower heard the soft start of a light rain. *Would there be a game tomorrow?*

Burley O'Malley walked into the room.

"Boss," he said in greeting.

"Burley," Tower replied.

As usual, he hadn't heard Burley coming up the stairs, but he wasn't surprised to see him. Another glass sat on the table. Burley poured himself a generous serving of beer. He could tell Tower was deep in thought. Tower, in turn, could tell Burley had something on his mind.

"What's up, Burley?" he asked. "What's bothering you?"

Burley mulled it over a moment before he spoke.

"Ezra Radford," he said. "He's been on my mind."

"What about him?"

"Something I can't quite figure out."

"What's that, Burley?"

"Well, he was the one who started the maps project, right?"

"That's right."

"He got in touch with Professor Watkins, got those kids sent to Spain to scout the coast."

Tower nodded, already sensing where Burley was going.

"Well," Burley continued, "you're the one who took things over after that. The admiral never actually got his hands on the final maps, did he? Not the real ones."

"No, Burley, he didn't."

"So I've just been wondering..." His voice trailed off.

"I know what you're wondering," Tower said, lifting his glass. "You're wondering why I stepped in when I did."

"Well, yeah—that's pretty much the full scale of my thinking."

Tower's voice dropped into a flat, matter-of-fact tone.

"It's because I didn't trust the admiral."

Burley said nothing. He simply looked at Tower and waited.

"A couple of months ago," Tower went on, "I learned the admiral had been sleeping with Julia Parrish. Whether his wife knew or only suspected it, I don't know. She idolized him. I never fully understood that until I saw it for myself."

He took a slow sip of beer.

"The problem was, he'd put himself in a position to be black-mailed. I didn't know that for certain at the time, but I strongly suspected it."

"And that's exactly what happened," Burley said.

Tower nodded. "Yes. And I think the worst came when the admiral realized Julia was working with the Spanish government. Instead of reporting it, he tried to go around her. He reached out to the Spanish directly—thought he could cut the Parrishes out of the deal."

"And that's why they killed him."

"I can't prove any of this," Tower said. "But it's the best explanation for what happened."

Burley considered this for a moment.

"So you decided that, since the admiral was already dead, he should be remembered as a hero—not a traitor?"

"There was some evidence in his office that he'd made contact with the Spanish. I found it and destroyed it," Tower said. "The man served this country for decades, and he did it well. He made one terrible mistake, and it cost him his life. But that shouldn't be his legacy."

Burley poured himself more beer.

The two men sat in silence, lost in their own thoughts about how the world really worked.

Epilogue

TWO DAYS AFTER THE meeting at the Douglass Café and Barbecue, Nathan Tower visited Lucinda and Meade Meadows at their home on Connecticut Avenue.

In a short, direct conversation, he asked them to join the Office of Naval Intelligence as permanent undercover operatives working directly under his command. With him, he brought commissioning documents granting them both the rank of First Lieutenant.

The Navy, of course, did not commission women—at least not officially—so Lucinda's document was issued under the name "L. C. Meadows."

Tower explained that Meade would continue in his role as a reporter at the *Washington Beacon*. Lucinda would continue her social and charitable engagements, maintaining her public role in Washington society.

Their commissions would never be made public. The documents would be secured in a classified naval vault at the Navy Yard in Washington.

Hubert Meadows was present when Tower made the offer. In fact, he had informed his children of the visit's purpose before the Commander arrived.

Lucinda and Meade accepted.

Together, they swore an oath to uphold and defend the Constitution of the United States against all enemies—foreign and domestic.

Tower smiled.

"Now," he said, "we have work to do."

About the author

Jim Stovall is the former Edward J. Meeman Distinguished Professor of Journalism at the University of Tennessee and professor emeritus at both the University of Alabama and the University of Tennessee. During his distinguished 30-year academic career, he specialized in writing, journalism, and public opinion research, teaching at institutions including the University of Alabama, Emory and Henry College, and the University of Tennessee.

Stovall is the author or co-author of numerous books, including *Writing for the Mass Media*, an introductory writing textbook used at more than 500 colleges and universities worldwide. His other works include *Seeing Suffrage: The Washington Suffrage Parade of 1913* (University of Tennessee Press), *Web Journalism: Practice and Promise of a New Medium*, and *Journalism: Who, What, Where, Why and How*. As a survey researcher and co-director of Southern Opinion Research, he conducted more than 200 public opinion surveys for clients including major newspapers and news organizations.

From 1970 to 1974, Stovall served on active duty in the United States Navy, where he was a staff writer for *All Hands* magazine. His journalism experience includes work with the Bristol Herald Courier, Knoxville News-Sentinel, Birmingham News, and Tuscaloosa News. He also worked as a graphics coordinator at the Chicago Tribune through fellowships from the American Society of Newspaper Editors.

A native of Nashville, Tennessee, Stovall earned his bachelor's degree in journalism from the University of Tennessee, his master's degree in political science from American University, and his doctorate in mass communication from the University of Tennessee.

The Death of the Admiral marks his debut in historical fiction, combining his expertise in American journalism and history with his lifelong fascination with espionage and intelligence operations. He lives in Tennessee with his wife Sally McMillan, where he spends his days reading, writing, painting watercolors, and trying to make each day better than the one before.

Live Your Values.
Value Your Life.

The Alignment Show: Real stories of realignment.

Hosted by "The Confidence Cultivator," Donn King, this podcast features conversations with people who've done the deep, sometimes scary work of bringing their lives into alignment with what matters most.

Some left jobs. Some stayed and reclaimed their joy. All faced a crossroads and chose to live with intention.

Are you wrestling with what really matters?

Are you ready to reconnect with what made you come alive?

Or do you simply want to hear from people who've been there?

Listen in. Be inspired. Begin again.

Find The Alignment Show on your favorite podcast app or visit TheAlignmentShow.com. (Scan this QR code → to listen or apply to be a guest).

> # "Nothing builds real confidence like living your values."

Ready to bring your book to life?

Donn offers independent publishing services for writers who want to retain creative control without sacrificing quality—covers, layout, consultation, and more.

Learn more at DonnKing.com/Admiral (or scan this QR code for more info →).